Just O

The King Family

Book 2

NEW YORK TIMES BESTSELLING AUTHOR

Carly Phillips

Print Edition

Cover Photo: Wander Aguiar
Cover Design: Maria @steamydesigns

* * *

JUST ONE SCANDAL

A jilted bride. Her brother's ex-buddy. An affair would be crazy…*right*?

Chloe Kingston's life is exactly how she needs it: safe and stable. Right up until her reliable, low-risk fiancé jilts her on their fairy-tale wedding day. As she works her way through the reception champagne—and wonders where she's going to live—she stumbles into her brother Linc's ex-best friend.

If only Beckett Daniels were hideous. But he's not. He's everything her erstwhile groom was not. Hot. Sexy. Dangerous. And she's just buzzed enough to want all that Greek-god gorgeousness to show her the kind of fun she's been missing.

Beck thrives on calculated risks, but taking advantage of Linc's little sister isn't one of them. What he can do is haul her tipsy, tulle-clad, tempting little butt to the bridal suite to sleep it off. Then move her into his spare room—which has the satisfying side effect of driving her brother crazy.

They can't remain platonic roommates for long. Not when the sexual attraction sizzles out of control. But when tragedy threatens Beck, pain from his past reminds them both that life doesn't come without risks…and this time, they're gambling with their hearts.

Chapter One

JILTED ON THE *day of my wedding. Of all the pathetic, clichéd things to happen*, Chloe Kingston thought with frustration and disgust. "How did I not see this coming?"

She fluffed her white ball gown dress, adjusting the tulle beneath the skirt, and sat down on the chair in the bridal suite of the hotel where her wedding was to be held.

She pulled a bottle of champagne out of the ice bucket and chugged down a healthy gulp of Dom Perignon straight from the bottle. Letting the bubbles settle, she repeated the action a couple of more times because she needed to get drunk. And on that thought, she took another hefty sip.

She was alone because she'd insisted she needed a few minutes by herself since getting *that* text. Her bridal party, consisting of her best friends, her sister, Aurora, and her brothers, because Owen had included them as his groomsmen, waited in the outer room. Impatiently if their loud voices were anything to go by. It had been hard to convince her mom to step out, along with her oldest brother, Linc, who Chloe had asked to walk her down the aisle.

Her father had passed away three months ago, and they hadn't been close. But she was glad he wasn't here to see this day. He'd be furious. Not because his daughter had been left at the altar but because he would have been embarrassed in front of friends, family, and business associates, and she couldn't deal with his reaction on top of everything else today. As it was, Chloe couldn't look at her mother's worried expression. Couldn't handle the pity in her friends' eyes or the fury in her brothers.

If there was one good thing about Owen ditching her via text message, it was that her brothers couldn't pound the man into the ground. And given the chance, they would. The Kingston siblings were nothing if not protective.

She glanced around the beautiful suite with plush chairs, makeup strewn around, her veil sitting on the counter, and wondered how she'd come to this point. She'd chosen who she thought was the perfect man. A tax attorney who never took risks, enjoyed staying home, and who'd promised to be faithful. He'd ticked off all the most important qualifications in her life, making her feel secure and comfortable and, most importantly, safe from being cheated on like her mother had been.

The screen on her phone sitting beside the headpiece said otherwise: *I'm sorry. I met someone who completes me. What I feel for her is more than two people who are comfortable together, like we are. I know I should have told you sooner. Face-to-face. But I really was going to marry you. Until I woke up this morning and just ... couldn't. Forgive me. I hope you find the love and excitement I have.*

Chloe's stomach twisted in a combination of hurt and embarrassment. Of all the cowardly actions ... that's what she got for choosing a man with a weak handshake who couldn't look her brothers in the eye. As they'd told her, over and over again, they hadn't thought Owen was good enough for her. But had she listened? Oh, no. She'd made her safe choice, and she'd intended to stick with her decision.

Had she loved Owen? Looking into her heart, she was forced to shake her head. No. She'd cared for him, that much was true. But love, like her brother and his best friend, Jordan, had found with each other? No, Chloe couldn't say she'd experienced that all-encompassing emotion.

In truth, love scared her, because her mom had loved her father so much she'd stayed in an extremely miserable marriage with a serial cheater and had lost out on the opportunity to embrace who she was and be happy. Maybe that was why Chloe was angry at Owen for how he'd handled things but not devastated over losing him.

Dammit. She lifted the bottle and took another long drink. She should have looked inward and called things off first, but who was she kidding? She never would have done it. Chloe was the good girl who always did the right thing, made the risk-free choices, and behaved as expected of her. Canceling the wedding wasn't something Chloe Kingston would ever have done.

A knock sounded loudly on the door, startling her. "Chloe? I'm coming in," her brother Linc called out.

She'd been alone in this room long enough, and she'd come to a decision, at least for tonight. It was time she told her family what she had planned.

"Okay!" she called out just as the door opened and Linc stepped inside, looking handsome in his black tuxedo. His gaze immediately zeroed in on the nearly empty champagne bottle in her hand.

"Not a word," she threatened him, waving the bottle in front of her. "I deserve this."

He nodded, his expression somber. "You do."

She lifted the bottle to her lips only to find it empty. Oh, well. There was more where this had come from. At least the bubbly liquid was beginning to do its trick, going to her head and lifting her mood.

Linc looked relieved and she chose not to enlighten him that, by the time the night was over, champagne would be the lightest drink she consumed.

"I'm sorry, Chloe. Owen's a bastard."

"Yes, he is. He should have told me sooner, and he should have done it in person. But he didn't and I have to handle the cards I've been dealt.

Linc nodded. "I'll go out and tell everyone to go home."

"No. Well, you can tell some of the guests to go home."

She pushed herself up from her chair and ignored the light spinning in her head. She hadn't had much to eat today, but there were appetizers galore almost ready to be served. At least that had been the post-ceremony agenda, followed by a three-course meal.

"What are you talking about?" Clearly concerned, Linc walked over and put a hand on her shoulder. "Mom wants you to come home with her. She and Aurora want to be there for you."

She thought about spending her wedding night in her mother's mansion-like house, her mom wringing her hands and trying not to cry for all Chloe had endured. "No. I want you to take Mom home. Take everyone in the family home." She stepped aside and his hand fell to his side.

Linc narrowed his gaze. "What about you?"

Her brother wasn't stupid and he knew her well. No doubt he saw the wheels in her mind spinning.

"You sublet your apartment and moved out. The boxes are in storage because you were supposed to live with Owen after your honeymoon." He winced at the mention of more plans that wouldn't be happening.

Plans she had no intention of thinking about yet.

Chloe drew a deep breath. "I have the honeymoon suite booked in the hotel tonight. I'll stay here. *After* my friends and I take advantage of the party that's already paid for. I'll just call it my non-wedding party." She let out a champagne-induced laugh and spun around, grabbing for the counter before she fell over.

"Chloe," Linc said in his stern, big-brother voice.

Ignoring him, she sat down, hiked up her gown, and unhooked the straps on her too-high-heeled, glittering sandals. "I can't dance in these," she said, kicking them across the room.

Her brother, who always had an answer and a solution, appeared concerned and at a loss. Before Chloe could reassure him, he strode to the door, pulled it open, and yelled for his fiancée. "Jordan! Get in here!"

"Reinforcements won't help," Chloe warned him, letting out another laugh, this one more of a giggle. Apparently she'd had more to drink than she'd realized, and she'd always been a lightweight.

Jordan, a gorgeous woman with jet-black hair, wearing an exquisite emerald-green gown, which Chloe knew had had to be let out to accommodate her early-pregnancy belly, rushed inside. "Is everything okay?"

"Chloe thinks she's going to party with her friends tonight. She wants her family to leave. Tell her she needs to go home with Mom and let us all take care of her," Linc ordered.

His frown would scare off most people, but Chloe had grown up with him. He'd do his best to exert his command, but she'd made up her mind. And he'd never been able to intimidate Jordan, who glanced at Chloe.

A silent understanding passed between them, woman to woman.

Jordan had grown up the daughter of the Kingston family's housekeeper, yet she and Linc had been best friends for years, and she'd been his personal assistant since he'd joined Kingston Enterprises after earning his MBA. Of everyone, Jordan knew how to handle him best. She always had.

And Jordan also understood the need to make her own choices. Chloe had faith her soon-to-be sister-in-law would support her.

"Linc," Jordan said, walking up to him and wrapping an arm around his waist. "I think Chloe knows what she needs. You can't just order her around and expect her to listen."

He blinked in shock. "You think her getting drunk is the answer to what happened here?" he asked.

"I think," Jordan said slowly, "it couldn't hurt. Let her do what she wants, and you can step in and play big brother tomorrow." She ran her hand over Linc's back. "I know you want to make it all better, but you can't. Not right now."

Chloe shot Jordan a grateful glance. "I owe you," she mouthed to her.

Chloe wished Jordan had taken her up on her offer to be a bridesmaid after she'd gotten engaged to Linc. But Jordan had issues with feeling like an outsider thanks to their very different backgrounds, and she felt she'd be coming in late and hadn't wanted to rock the boat. Chloe intended to make Jordan feel more like family than the closest family member. She still would do that after she celebrated her un-wedding.

"I don't like this," Linc muttered.

"You don't have to." Jordan tugged on his hand. "Let's go talk to the family." She glanced at Chloe. "Who do you want me to send in to be with you?"

Chloe forced a smile. "Send my bridesmaids in, please. And tell anyone who isn't family that wants to stay and party to stick around." She would enjoy tonight if it killed her.

"Chloe, why don't you let us stay, too?" Linc asked, attempting to handle things one last time.

"Because you'd all kill my fun. You'd sit around with concerned looks, waiting for me to fall apart. And

I'd be worried about all of you, and that would defeat the purpose of a party." The explanation made sense to her.

"Linc, come." Jordan tugged at his hand, and soon she'd led him out of the room.

But not before he stopped, walked over to Chloe, and pulled her into a brotherly hug. "You deserve the very best, and I promise you the right person is out there. I love you, Chlo."

She tightened her arms around him, accepting the love she'd never gotten from her father. "I love you, too. Just let me have this night. Tomorrow is soon enough to face things."

Linc groaned. "Okay, Scarlett O'Hara. But we will talk then."

Of that, Chloe had no doubt.

In the morning, Linc would do his best to take over, and she'd just have to deal with him then. God, she adored her family. Her love life might suck, but she had a support system not many people could claim. The problem was, come tomorrow, she'd be smothered in worry by well-meaning relatives.

But tonight was for her.

After watching Linc and Jordan walk out, Chloe rose and dug for the ballet flats she'd planned to wear once her feet began to hurt. She slipped them on so she could dance. After all, they'd paid for a high-priced

DJ, and she intended to enjoy every moment until she crashed. There might come a time when she cried, but she refused to think about her pain.

Just then, her friends piled into the room, and she braced herself to explain her plans for the evening one more time.

Then they'd have fun.

★ ★ ★

"HAPPY BIRTHDAY TO you. Happy birthday to you. Happy birthday, dear Dad, happy birthday to you." Beckett Daniels's family finished singing to their father and followed the lyrics with a round of applause.

"Make a wish, Kurt," Audrey, Beck's mom, said to her husband.

He looked around at his wife, Beck, and his other two sons, Drew and Tripp, and smiled, the gratitude in his expression obvious. Then he paused and blew out the candles.

Beck wondered, as he did every year, if his father wished for everyone sitting at this table's health and well-being. God knows that was Beck's annual birthday prayer. They'd all learned years ago how fragile life could be after losing Tripp's twin, Whitney, when they were teens.

The server reached over and lifted the cake. "We'll slice it and be right back. I'll take your coffee orders then," he said and walked away.

"I don't know about you but that cake looked delicious," his mother said. "And that frosting? Mmm. I can't wait."

Tripp, a pediatrician, grinned. "I'll take a big chunk, myself."

Andrew glanced at their father. "You look like you could use a slice, Dad. Have you lost weight?"

Beck shifted his gaze back to his father, noting the more drawn look in his lower face. "Now that Drew's mentioned it, you do look thinner."

His father waved a hand through the air. "I'm finc, boys. Don't worry about me."

Beck always worried. But tonight they were at his father's favorite steak restaurant. There might have been a time the Daniels family couldn't afford a restaurant this fancy or expensive, and Beck and his brothers had put themselves through school on loans, but they'd always had love. And now Beck, Tripp, or Drew could more than cover the cost of taking their parents out for an extravagant dinner.

His father looked up, his eyes widening. "And there's our dessert."

Beck tried to get his mother's attention to see if she'd give him an inkling about his dad's health, but she was busy digging into the cake the server had placed in front of her first. He held back a groan, telling himself he shouldn't jump to conclusions. It wasn't like he spent all his time thinking about his sister, but she was always there, ready to pop into his mind and remind him how quickly things could change. How fast life could turn to loss.

"Beck? I asked if you'd like a piece?" his mom asked.

He nodded, knowing it would make her happy. "Hit me up," he said. "And make it a big slice." Pushing sad thoughts out of his head, he focused on enjoying the here and now. Something he was still learning how to do, many, many years later. Losing a sibling to leukemia had been harsh and difficult, and they all still suffered the aftereffects all this time later.

"Hey, when we finish eating, who wants to head to the bar downstairs and have a drink?" Drew, the lawyer in the family, asked.

"I'm in," Tripp said, shoveling the cake in his mouth as he spoke.

Laughing, Beck lifted a piece onto his fork. "I'll join you," he said, then took the cake into this mouth. The chocolate melted and he damn near moaned out loud. "This is amazing," he said, going in for another bite.

"Mom? Dad?" Tripp turned their way. "Want to come?"

"Oh, no. You boys stay out and have some fun.

We're just going to go home like the old people we are." She grinned and they all rolled their eyes.

His mom had married his father after she'd graduated college. Then she'd gotten pregnant with Drew at the age of twenty-three. Now fifty-eight, she looked a lot younger than her years. Nobody would call either of his parents *old.* But if they wanted to go home, everyone understood.

A little while later, with the check taken care of and goodbyes said to their parents, Beck, Tripp, and Drew made their way out of the restaurant and headed toward the main lobby bar.

A nighttime hotspot, the lobby was crowded, people lining up past the entrance and mingling in the main room and around the fountain in the center.

"I guess we're not getting near the drinks any time soon," Drew muttered.

"Doesn't seem like it." Tripp stopped walking so they could talk and regroup.

"Do you want to go somewhere else? Or we could head back to my apartment and have a few drinks there." Beck didn't care as long as he spent time with his siblings.

"Your place sounds good. I'm not looking to pick anyone up tonight," Drew said.

"I'll get us an Uber." Tripp pulled out his cell.

They began to head toward the side entrance

where it was quieter and they could more easily locate their ride share when a burst of feminine laughter caught Beck's attention.

He glanced up in time to see a bride walking across the lobby, surrounded by three other women in matching dresses.

"Gives a whole other meaning to women going to the ladies' room together," Beck said to his brothers.

Tripp laughed only to be tag teamed by two of the bridesmaids.

"Ooh, you're cute," a pretty brunette said.

"I saw him first, Wendy. Go find your own guy." The proprietary woman grabbed Tripp's elbow and hung on tight.

Beck's sibling raised his eyebrows but didn't attempt to disengage his new appendage.

"I'll take this one then." The woman with auburn hair latched on to Drew.

Beck didn't know whether to be insulted or relieved that none of the women had chosen him.

"I know you!" The bride, who had obviously gotten waylaid because she just joined them now, tripped and fell against Beck's chest.

He braced his hands on her bare forearms, steadying her as he helped her stand up straight. When she didn't wobble, he released her and met her gaze. Long blond hair fell in waves around her exquisite face, and blue eyes with a darker rim around the edges stared back at him, reminding him of someone he knew.

"Beckett Daniels, right?" she asked.

"Yes." There was a familiarity to her features. He knew her, he just couldn't place her. "And you're..."

"Chloe Kingston. Linc's sister." She treated him to a megawatt smile that had the power to knock him on his ass.

Son. Of. A. Bitch. Linc, his one-time best friend. Now a man he barely spoke to.

"You and my brother are business competitors," she said and let out a little hiccup. Clearly she was as drunk as her bridesmaids.

"That would be putting it mildly." But he wasn't about to elaborate on his relationship with her brother. If Linc hadn't seen fit to tell her the sordid details, he wasn't going to go there, either. It was a time in his life he'd much rather forget.

Looking at Chloe, her flushed cheeks, in her inebriated state, he assumed the ceremony had already taken place. "So you kept your maiden name?" he asked. Because she hadn't introduced herself as Chloe Kingston Something-or-Other.

"Oh, no. No, no, no." She waved her hand through the air, her long nails a pale white color. "I'm not married." A deeper flush rose to her face. "I was left at the altar."

Beck blinked, then stared at her, stunned. "What kind of asshole would stand up a gorgeous woman like you?" Despite her relation to his sworn enemy, Beck couldn't deny the fact that the girl he'd met in college was all grown up and one hell of a knockout.

"You're sweet." She sniffed and he was afraid he'd triggered a crying jag, but she forced a smile instead. "He found someone who *completes him*," she said, using quotation marks with her fingers. "And he hopes I *find the love and excitement he has*." She finished with more finger quotes.

She sniffed again. "But the bastard did it by text. And I'm celebrating because everything is paid for, and I think just maybe he did me a favor. Even if I sometimes want to cry." She fluttered her thick black lashes, and Beck was afraid she'd do just that.

He didn't know what to make of Chloe or what to do with her. On the one hand, he wanted to beat the crap out of the man who'd hurt her. On the other, he needed to remember she was Linc's sister and he ought to stay far away.

"Anyway." Chloe interrupted his train of thought, which was going in a direction he didn't like but which still held some appeal. "I figured why let everything go to waste? So we're partying! Come with me!" she said, tugging on his sleeve.

He glanced at his brothers, who were preoccupied

with her bridesmaids, and rolled his eyes. No matter what they decided to do, he was not going in there and dealing with her brother.

"I don't think that's a good idea."

Her wide smile dimmed. "Why not? You want to dump me, too?" Her pout was too fucking adorable, and her words hit him in the gut.

"No, I don't want to dump a beautiful … umm … bride like you. But Linc and I aren't on the best of terms."

"Oh!" Her smile returned. "Well, that's no problem. Linc's not here. I made my family go home. I didn't want to see their sad, worried faces at my non-wedding party." She flung her arm, gesturing toward the double doors on the far side of the lobby.

"Your brother left you drunk after being … well, he just left?" Beck stopped himself before he reminded her she'd been dumped.

Still, he was shocked. She had three brothers. If she were *his* sister, no way would Beck have abandoned her on a night like this. Then again, *his* sister wouldn't have the opportunity to fall in love or get married, though it had been on the bucket list she'd made near the end. A list of experiences she wished she could have and ones she wanted Beck to enjoy in her place.

"Come dance with me." Chloe slipped her soft

hand into his, raised his arm, and twirled around until dizziness had her crashing into him once more.

He found himself wrapping an arm around her waist and hauling her sweet curves against him. Inhaling, he took in her delectable, warm scent and wanted to bury his face in her neck and nibble on her fragrant skin. His cock jerked in agreement.

"What do you say? Are we going to party with the ladies?" Tripp asked, glancing at Drew, his arm around the brunette, before looking back at Beck.

His brothers, like Beck, dated without thinking about settling down. They probably saw these women as easy pickings.

Beck felt Chloe's body, soft and warm against his. He glanced down and her gorgeous eyes stared back at him, those lips puckered up like she was waiting for a kiss.

Jesus. How could he send her off to continue getting wasted on her own? At least that's the excuse he gave himself when he nodded at his brother and said, "Why not? Let's go party."

"Yay!" Chloe clapped her hands, her pleasure obvious. Then she grasped his hand and led him toward the ballroom, his brothers and their women following.

The room had been decked out for a gala. Between the flowers, the décor, the gold chairs, and the centerpieces, no money had been spared. His heart hurt for the drunk would-have-been bride. He might despise her brother, but Beck wouldn't blame his sister for Linc's actions or wish bad things on other people in their family.

"Let's dance," she said and, without waiting for him, sashayed onto the makeshift dance floor.

Before deciding whether or not to join her, he watched as she began to sway to the music, her body coming alive to the beat. A veritable princess in her ballroom gown. What kind of asshole would dump this woman? From being in the real estate business, he was aware of her job as Kingston Enterprises' lead decorator. She furnished any building purchased or leased out by Kingston Enterprises, and though their aesthetic was more staid than what Beck and his company preferred, Chloe was clearly beautiful as well as talented.

And the Kingston family, like Beck himself, was often the subject of tabloid gossip about the rich and famous. Which meant the devastation she was trying so hard to hide would soon be public knowledge. There was no avoiding that.

Maybe he should help her enjoy the night before she had to face her future. He stepped toward the dance floor just as another man joined her and pulled her to him, obviously grinding against her. She braced her hands on his shoulders in a clear attempt to push him away.

Beck rushed forward and shoved at the guy's shoulder, breaking his hold on Chloe.

"What the fuck?" the man asked, his gaze going from the woman in the wedding gown to Beck. "She invited me. She came into the bar earlier and said she wants to party. I was just showing her a good time."

Beck frowned, realizing Chloe's *non-wedding* could get out of hand. "Well, she changed her mind, and she isn't interested in what you're offering. Get lost or I'll have you thrown out."

"I don't need this shit." The guy glared at Chloe before he turned and strode out.

One crisis averted, Beck thought.

Chloe grasped his arm and sighed. "Thank you. You're my hero!" She lifted her arms and flung herself against him, giving him a nose full of her fruity-smelling hair. Once again her soft curves crushed his chest, tempting him, and his dick reacted.

Down, boy, he thought, because Chloe was in no frame of mind to fall into bed with a virtual stranger. It would be no better than taking advantage of her, and Beck would never stoop so low. Not to mention, he'd had a sister and he'd kick the ass of anyone who'd exploited her.

He looked overhead and saw his brothers having fun with the bridesmaids. They seemed fine and could take care of themselves. Catching Tripp's gaze, he mouthed he was leaving and his brother nodded.

Beck braced his hands on Chloe's waist and eased her away from him, looking into her glassy eyes. Yep, time to get this bride to bed.

"Come on, princess," he said because that's what she resembled. A fairy-tale princess. "Time to go. I'll take you home."

Her lower lip trembled, the first sign of outward fragility and hurt she'd shown since targeting him in the lobby. "I don't have a home. All my things are in boxes. I was going to move them into Owen's house after the wedding."

"Owen the douchebag, huh? Okay, then how about your mom's?" Her father had passed away a few months ago from a heart attack. While most people in the industry had shown up for the funeral, Beck had passed.

"Owen the douchebag." She giggled at his description. "And no, I'm not going to my mother's with my tail between my legs like a little girl." She shook her head back and forth. "Nope. Not happening."

He groaned. "One of your brothers, then?" And he'd better not have to show up with her on Linc's doorstep.

She shook her head again, her expression adamant. "Either they'll say I told you so or they'll hover."

Obviously neither option appealed to her.

"Don't worry though. I have a plan," she said, surprising him. "We'd rented the honeymoon suite for the night. I'll just crash there."

She started to walk away, but if this were a sobriety test, she'd fail in a heartbeat. She wobbled her first few steps, tripped, and he darted forward, making a split-second decision before she took a header onto the floor. Lifting her, he adjusted her until she was more secure. Her delicate arms wrapped around him, and she buried her face in the crook of his neck and shoulder.

"I'm tired." Her lips moved against his skin, her breath warm against his flesh.

At the arousing sensation, his entire body shook with need. "Fuck," he muttered as he walked, ignoring the stares as he carried her out of the ballroom.

"Can we?" she asked without lifting her head from his shoulder.

He stifled a groan. "No. You're going to go upstairs to pass out cold." Another man, the man he wished he could be, would take advantage of her just to show Linc Kingston what betrayal felt like.

But Beck had been raised right.

He stopped at the front desk and roused Chloe long enough for her to ask for her room key. Obviously they already knew her, and the bridal dress pretty much said it all. The man behind the counter handed over the key. And Beck made his way upstairs with the passed-out-again bride in his arms.

Chapter Two

SOMEHOW BECK MANAGED to open the door to the suite, carry Chloe inside, and finally set her down on the bed. She seemed to fall asleep immediately, her ball gown spread across the mattress, her ballet-slipper-covered feet peeking out from the hem. He slipped off the shoes and stared down at the passed-out bride.

He could leave her alone to sleep it off, but she might wake up frightened and not remember how she'd gotten here. His conscience told him not to abandon her on what was supposed to be her wedding night. After another glance at the vulnerable woman, he headed to the bathroom. The large counter with double sinks was also full of amenities, and he was able to brush his teeth before heading back inside.

Instead of still being passed out, she was sitting up in bed, surrounded by the layers of her gown, with mascara-stained tears streaming down her face.

Aww, shit. Now he had a crying female on his hands. He turned back to the bathroom, coming out with a box of tissues in his hand. He approached the bed and extended his arm so she could grab a Kleenex.

"Thank you." She pulled three sheets from the box and dabbed at her eyes, succeeding only in smearing the makeup around her face.

Settling on the side of the bed, he took her chin in one hand and, with a tissue, gently blotted and wiped the black stains off her soft skin.

"You're so nice," she said and immediately began crying again, which meant he had to begin all over cleaning her up.

Knowing she was drunk and the alcohol was exacerbating her shitty feelings, Beck let her continue to sob it out. There was nothing else he could do.

"I don't get how I could have screwed up so badly. I picked the nice guy, the safe guy, the guy who I thought would never screw me over like my father did to my mom. And here I am, alone on my wedding night." She lifted her hands and helplessly dropped them back to her lap and continued to list all the reasons she'd chosen her groom.

Not one of them, he noted, was love.

The longer she spoke, the more her hysteria built, and Beck sat back to let her get it all out, only reaching out occasionally to dab at the dripping black tears in order to save the white gown from ruin. If anyone had told him this was how he'd be spending his night, he'd have had a good, hard laugh. The fact that it was Linc

Kingston's sister made it even more ironic.

"We even liked to stay in at night and watch television together," she said on a wail. "It's not like he was a guy who chose bars and drinking. So much for playing it safe."

"Safe isn't always smart," he said, handing her another tissue.

She blotted her eyes and nose, then handed him back the Kleenex. He shook his head and put it on the dresser.

"And now I'm stuck with no place to live and a boring job with a brother I love but who won't let me branch out and … and … what happened to my life?" she asked. She glanced down and started to work an emerald-shaped engagement ring off her finger.

"Wait. Stop." He didn't need that expensive rock lost somewhere in this hotel room. "Leave it on until you can put it somewhere safe. Then you can decide what to do with it."

"I hate looking at it," she said. Even pouting, she was pretty.

Knowing he was in way over his head, the best thing he could do was get her to fall back to sleep. She'd wake up in the morning no happier, but at least she'd be sober, and, he assumed, calmer.

"Listen, I think you should get some rest. Things will look brighter tomorrow. What do you say?"

She nodded and then, taking him off guard, pushed herself around him to the end of the bed and rose to her feet. Stepping over, she turned her back toward him and lifted her heavy, gorgeous hair and swept it to one side.

"Undo my buttons," she demanded.

"What? Why?"

She turned her head, giving him a perfect view of her exquisite profile. "Because you said I should go to sleep, and I can't get comfortable in this dress."

He swallowed a curse. She had a point, but that meant he'd be left with Chloe sleeping in whatever she had on beneath that dress while he … what? Sat in the uncomfortable chair in the corner? Or stretched out beside her and ignored his aching cock.

"Fine," he said through gritted teeth. It took a while for his big fingers to slip each tiny button through the small loops, but he finally managed, revealing inch after inch of her porcelain skin. "All set," he muttered.

"Whew!" She released her hair, and as it tumbled down her back, she shrugged and let the dress fall to the floor before spinning back to face him.

She stood in a strapless white lace push-up bra, sexy matching panties, and a blue garter hooked around her thigh. She was a vision with her blond hair tumbling over her shoulders and the body of a goddess.

He swallowed a low groan of desire just as she reached for the back hook of her bra.

"No!" He couldn't handle it if she stripped down to nothing, and there was no way she'd be happy with herself in the morning. "Climb into bed. I'm sure you'll be comfortable like that."

She pouted but did as he asked, striding to the other side of the mattress, giving him a view of her heart-shaped ass in the barely there panties. He shook his head, wondering what he'd done in this lifetime to deserve such torture.

She turned down the covers, slid beneath, and he gave a relieved sigh. That is, until she wriggled under the comforter and the bra went flying across the room, followed by the garter. As he braced himself for her panties to go next, she lay her head on the pillow, sighed, closed her eyes, and just like that, fell asleep.

His shoulders dropped as his tension eased, and Beck let out a long groan of relief. Now that he didn't have a hysterical woman to deal with, he turned his attention to where he'd be spending the night. One look at the uncomfortable chair and he nixed that idea. He'd just have to lie on top of the covers with as much space between him and Chloe as he could manage.

After kicking off his shoes, he sat on the side of the bed and took off his socks and shirt, laying them on the chair he'd opted not to sleep on. After debating, he said fuck it and removed his jeans. His boxer briefs were good enough.

Then he climbed on the bed. Using the bedspread that had fallen to the floor as a blanket, he pulled it over himself and settled back against the pillows on his side of the bed. Beside him, Chloe let out little snores that had him grinning despite the situation.

Being with Chloe Kingston brought back memories he'd always done his best to keep far away. He'd met Linc in college. They'd been roommates and become best friends. While Linc had a family who could pay for everything, giving him time to party as well as study, Beck had attended partially on scholarship but mostly on loans, and he'd had to work for spending money. By sophomore year, he and Linc had formed a tight bond. Took the same classes, had the same life goals, and had found girlfriends at the same time. They'd gone out together as couples and hung out at parties.

Beck remembered how much his girlfriend, Jenna, resented his need to work because it meant they couldn't spend as much time together as Linc and his girlfriend, Lacey, did. She was jealous and Beck knew it, but there was nothing he could do, and he would placate her until she calmed down.

Everything was great until one night when Beck

worked late and came home to find Linc and who he thought was Linc's girlfriend in bed together. No sooner had Beck shut the door than Jenna sat up, looked at him, and began to cry about how she was sorry and they hadn't meant for it to happen. Even remembering that moment now, Beck saw red, his anger stemming as much from Jenna's hurt and betrayal as it had from Linc's. Maybe more so from Linc because nobody did that to his best friend.

He glanced over at the still-snoring woman beside him, nearly naked beneath the covers. Beck had a cutthroat reputation in business. He'd had to be smart and fast if he was going to make the kind of money he'd craved in a business he hadn't been born into like Linc had been. Beck had accomplished his goals, exceeding beyond his wildest imaginings by never showing weakness and always using situations to his advantage. But that reputation didn't extend to women.

Another guy might use Linc's sister to get payback. Not Beck. Chloe was safe with him. And Linc Kingston ought to thank his lucky stars that Beck had morals. More so than Linc himself had had back when they were friends.

He closed his eyes and listened to the rhythmic breathing Chloe had fallen into and drifted off to sleep. Beck wasn't sure how much time had passed when loud knocking sounded, waking him from a not-so-great sleep.

He glanced around the room, taking in his surroundings and remembering where he was and who was in bed beside him. Thanks to his remaining above the comforter, they hadn't rolled against each other during the night, but she had moved closer and he inhaled her fragrant scent.

The knock that must have woken him sounded again.

Chloe groaned and shifted to her side. No doubt she would be hurting this morning.

The pounding continued and Beck slid out of bed, heading for the door to ask housekeeping to come back later. Who else could be there at this hour?

He wasn't about to open the door, either. Neither he nor Chloe was dressed.

"Chloe? Open up!" a familiar male voice called out as Beck touched the doorknob.

Linc. Well, this was about to get interesting.

Not caring what Linc thought, Beck drew a deep breath and opened the door for his former friend.

Linc took one look at Beck and his mouth opened in shock. "What the fuck are you doing here?" Before Beck could answer, Linc brushed past him and walked into the outer room of the suite. "I swear to God if you took advantage of my sister, I'll kill you."

Beck let the door shut behind them before turning to Linc with a scowl.

Meanwhile, Linc's hands curled into fists at his sides, reminding Beck of how he'd taken a swing at Linc after finding him in bed with Jenna. "Taking advantage of women is more your style than mine."

Linc jerked at the insult. "This isn't about what happened back then. I left Chloe here against my better judgment, and it turns out I was right." Linc's gaze raked over Beck's lack of clothing. "Where's my sister?"

"In bed." Beck couldn't help tossing out the words that would rile Linc up more. But before he could react, Beck continued. "You're just damned lucky I was there to make sure she got up here safely."

Linc's jaw locked in place, and he visibly drew a calming breath. "She's not safe if she's with you."

Beck laughed but it was harsh. "It's not like you were there to look out for her."

Linc stepped forward, clearly planning to swing, and Beck was ready.

"Linc, stop!" Chloe's voice had both men turning toward her.

She'd obviously found the hotel robe before coming out here, because she was tying the belt around her waist as she stood there, facing them. Her hair was a wild tangle around her face, and despite the crying jags last night, he'd obviously managed to clean her up fairly well. There were black circles under her eyes, but her cheeks weren't smudged with makeup. Just flushed with embarrassment but still just as attractive, if not more so now that he saw her softer, real side.

"Are you okay?" Linc stepped toward her but she held him off with her hand in the air.

She nodded. "I'm fine. What are you doing here?"

He narrowed his gaze. "I think the better question is what are you doing with him?"

"If you must know, I drank too much and he … umm … helped me up here." Her cheeks burned brighter and she couldn't meet Beck's gaze.

"That better be all he did," Linc muttered. "Come on, Chloe. Let's go."

"What?" She straightened her shoulders.

"You can come stay with me and Jordan until you get yourself sorted out."

She shook her head the way she had last night when Beck had suggested nearly the same thing. "No. You two have a baby on the way. You're new as a couple. You need your time together. I won't be a third wheel. And before you say Mom's, I won't go there, either. Or Xander's or Dash's place. Just no." She wrapped her arms around herself, looking lost.

Most likely because, as she'd told Beck, she'd given up her apartment and really did have nowhere to go.

"You can stay with me." The words were out before he could stop them or even think them through.

But he had to admit Linc's horror-filled expression made the offer worth it. "I have plenty of room at my place and you won't be in the way. You can stay until you make a plan of your own."

Chloe shot him a look filled with surprise and some gratitude. "I–"

"No. He's just using you to get back at me," Linc said. "I won't have it."

Chloe drew herself up tall, and Beck knew immediately Linc had made his final mistake.

"*You won't have it?* Well, it's not your decision to make." She strode up to her brother and got in his personal space. "I don't know what went on between you and Beck and I don't care. What I do know is that he was there for me last night, and since he's still willing to help, I'm going to take him up on his offer. Now it's time for you to go." She turned away from Linc, strode to the door, and held it open.

Linc briefly closed his eyes, then opened them again. "I'm sorry. I know it's your choice, but please let your family be the ones to help."

She shook her head. "I need time to sort out my life without anyone else telling me what they think is best."

"I understand that but with him? Not to mention,

I came to tell you that the society pages of the papers and social media sites picked up the story." His tone gentled as he broke the news.

"Great." She pressed her hands to cheeks that had flushed in embarrassment. "So now I'm a public laughingstock."

Linc shook his head. "I'm sorry. Since Dad died and some asshole named you the Kingston heiress, people have kept an eye on your engagement."

Beck felt sorry for her, being in a spotlight she hadn't asked for, but it came along with her family's wealth.

"Well, I'm taking my honeymoon time off from work, so that should help me stay out of sight and make people forget about me. Now, go home to Jordan. Please." She swept her arm toward the hallway.

Linc shot Beck a warning glare before walking toward the door. He braced a hand on the frame and turned. "Chloe, I love you and just want what's best for you." *And Beck isn't it* resounded without him saying the actual words.

"Then let me make those decisions for myself," Chloe said, and Linc finally listened to her and walked out the door.

★ ★ ★

WITH HER BROTHER gone, Chloe groaned and laid her

pounding head on her arm against the doorframe, unable and unwilling to face her so-called savior just yet. What she hadn't said out loud, wasn't willing to admit, was that she couldn't remember anything past Beck carrying her upstairs and placing her on the bed.

She'd woken up to the sound of the two men yelling and realized she wore only her underwear beneath the covers of the hotel bed. Then she'd grabbed a robe and entered the main room to find Beck, one fine male specimen, wearing boxer briefs and nothing more.

"Chloe?" Beck's voice called to her.

Knowing she had no choice, she straightened and turned to face him. "Hi."

He grinned at her. "Hi."

She bit the inside of her cheek and forced herself to ask the question she needed the answer to more than any other. "What happened last night? I don't remember beyond you bringing me up here. Thank you, by the way. But did we…" A raging flush rose to her cheeks.

"Relax, princess. Nothing happened except I brought you up here and put you to bed."

"Princess?"

His low, sexy laugh made her body parts tingle. "That's what you looked like in your gown."

"Umm … did you undress me?" she forced herself to ask.

He folded his arms across his chest, his muscles bunching in his forearms, his six-pack hard and firm. Never mind the bulge in his boxer briefs she was trying hard not to look at.

"I unhooked all those buttons. You did the strip-tease yourself." He winked and she burned all over.

"I'm so embarrassed." She placed her hands on her hot cheeks.

"Don't be. Considering the day you'd had, I think you held up well. Except for the crying about how your safe choice in men turned out to be anything but."

She winced, the memories of how she'd behaved coming back to her in flashes. "Oh, God."

"It's fine. Everything will work out," he assured her. And when he said it, she almost believed him.

"Come on." He grasped her elbow. "Let's look at the room service menu. I'm sure you need something to eat. Then we can head back to my place."

Her head jerked up. Though she'd told Linc she'd take Beck up on his offer to stay with him, she was far from having decided that yet. She'd just wanted her brother to give her time and space.

"I don't know if that's a good idea."

He raised an eyebrow. "Do you have anywhere else to go?"

"Well, no. Unless I take a hotel room." She didn't

want a cold, sterile place to stay any more than she wanted her family's worried looks and attempts at help.

He shrugged. "Your choice but I have a spare guest room, and the invitation's open."

"I'll take it," she said before she could change her mind. "I just have one request."

"Name it," he said.

"You can't walk around in your underwear."

He burst out laughing and the sight was incredible. He was so handsome with his jet-black hair on the longer side, his jade-green eyes and sculpted features. And when he let go enough to laugh like that? She was drawn to him even more.

But her brother obviously had issues with the man. She knew they were business rivals and also recalled them being friends in college until they'd had some sort of falling-out. Linc never talked about it. And for today, she didn't want to know the details.

But there was something she was curious about. "Beck? Why did you help me last night?"

His expression grew more serious. "At first you'd just pulled us in to have fun. Once I realized how much you'd had to drink and when I saw someone make a play for you, I decided someone needed to keep you safe. I didn't want anyone taking advantage." He shrugged as if it were no big deal.

But to her it was. He clearly could have had sex with her and left her alone in that big bed. But he hadn't. "And why did you stay?"

He ran a hand over his face. "I didn't want you to wake up alone and be scared. I'm going to get the menu," he said and disappeared into the other room.

Clearly she'd made him uncomfortable. Still, warmth settled in her chest, and gratitude that he was a decent guy rushed over her. She knew his business reputation and had heard Linc cursing over lost deals to Beck's company more than once. So maybe he was a shark in the boardroom.

But he'd definitely been a saint in the bedroom. Since she'd been drunk, she was thankful. But she couldn't help wondering what sex with Beck would be like if she were sober. Something a woman who'd been dumped not twenty-four hours ago shouldn't be thinking about.

She ought to be beside herself with grief, pain, and hurt. Instead she was pissed and embarrassed, especially since the social media poster who'd dubbed her the Kingston heiress was someone she'd dumped after two dates. He'd started his site after they'd broken up, and because his sense of humor was dry and he was good-looking, people gravitated to him, and he'd gone viral. Well, whatever. She didn't care what anyone thought. She just didn't want pity.

She could take a step back now and admit that she'd never reacted to Owen's body the way she did to Beck's. Never imagined getting sweaty between the sheets with her own fiancé. Sex between them was perfunctory at best. Definitely not mind-blowing or life-altering. And something told her that tangling with Beck would be all those things and more.

Catching herself thinking about Beck again, she shook her head and reminded herself they were acquaintances. He was doing her a favor, giving her a place to stay, and she ought to appreciate him for that. Besides, it wasn't like he was ogling her body, which was too bad. But still, she needed to focus on herself and her future.

She and Beck were going to be roommates. Nothing more.

★ ★ ★

AFTER INDULGING IN a delicious breakfast of pure carbs that helped her hangover, Chloe took a long, hot shower. She lathered away yesterday's mess and washed the hairspray out of her hair with the hotel-provided shampoo. She used their conditioner, as well, and somehow managed to finger comb her long strands before pulling them up with a hair tie into a messy bun.

Before she'd gotten into the shower, the hotel had

sent her belongings from the bridal room upstairs, giving her the basics she'd brought with her yesterday along with the carry-on suitcase she'd left with the concierge for her overnight stay here.

She changed into the outfit she'd planned on wearing for the flight to Maui that wouldn't be happening: a pair of taupe jersey-knit leggings, a matching fitted tank top, a cardigan, and her favorite snakeskin boots. She refused to think about the fact that she and Owen were supposed to be enjoying their honeymoon together. Somehow in the time since he'd texted her and now, her concerns were more about where she'd take her life from here and not about how sad she was over losing her future husband.

She already understood she'd had a lucky escape with Owen finding what everyone *should* look for in a partner. How and when he'd handled the breakup, however, was what upset her. She'd have to send back wedding and engagement gifts, and her mother would go through the ordeal of explaining the end of their engagement and non-wedding to people. Not to mention the money wasted. God, Owen was an ass, and Chloe wished she could sue him for the cost but knew she never would.

When she walked out of the bedroom, she found Beck on the phone, looking out the window at the Manhattan view below. He wore his clothes from last night, a pair of dark fitted jeans that molded to his incredible body, tight ass, and thighs and a light blue men's dress shirt, untucked, on top.

"Still at the hotel," he said into his cell. "That's right." He listened, then said, "None of your goddamned business, Tripp. Talk to you later." He disconnected the call.

"Hey," she said, joining him.

He turned. "Hey yourself. Feel better?" he asked.

She nodded. "More like myself."

"Well, you look better, if you don't mind my saying so." His gaze skimmed the length of her body, obviously taking in and appreciating her curves if the glimmer in his eyes was anything to go by.

Her body reacted to his appraisal, her nipples tightening beneath her bra. She refused to glance down and see if it was noticeable.

She forced a smile at him. "I'm pretty sure the black mascara running down my cheeks wasn't my finest moment." Neither was how she'd unloaded all her emotional drama on him, but since he hadn't brought it up again, neither would she.

He slid his hands into his front pants pockets and chuckled. "You deserved a good cry."

"Which I apparently had." She winced at the memories that had come back to her. "You went above and beyond for someone you don't know, and I can't tell you how much I appreciate it," she said. Whatever had gone down with Linc, Chloe would always think Beck was a great guy.

"Ready to go check out your new digs?" he asked. "I live in a renovated loft downtown."

She raised her eyebrows. "Oooh, sounds awesome." She couldn't wait to see it. "Are you one-hundred-percent certain you don't mind the company?"

He strode over until they were close and dipped his head. "Your memories seem to have returned. You remember how I brought you here?"

She smelled the minty toothpaste on his breath. "You carried me up here."

"Right. So if you keep asking if it's okay, I'm going to have to resort to the same caveman approach." He rose to his full height. "In other words, don't test me."

A weight lifted off her chest. "Okay then. Let's go."

On the way downtown in an Uber, Chloe called her mother and checked in, assured her she was staying with a friend, and promised to keep in touch. And once her honeymoon vacation time was over, she would deal with wrapping up the remnants of her non-wedding.

Chapter Three

BECK WORRIED ABOUT the woman who walked silently beside him down the hall to his loft. She'd been just as quiet on the ride here. He understood she had a lot to think about and deal with, so he gave her the space to do that, but he was aware of her the entire trip. They sat close in the back seat of an Uber, the mint scent of the hotel shampoo tickling his nose and the constant fiddling of her hands drawing his attention.

"Here we are." He stopped at the double entry doors that opened to his place, used his cell phone app to undo the lock and, once they entered, unarmed the alarm. "Welcome," he said, pulling the suitcase he'd insisted on carrying inside.

Chloe stepped in behind him, her eyes lighting up as she looked around. "Wow. This place is incredible!"

"Thank you." He knew what she saw, a view straight across the dark hardwood floor to windows rounded on top and surrounded by brick on each wall, overlooking downtown. Comfortable cream chairs, an L-shaped sofa, and a leather ottoman with live plants filled one corner of the living room. A foosball table sat against a wall, and a makeshift bar was in another corner.

Was it a bachelor pad? Pretty much. But he figured he'd earned it. The loft, along with his Midtown offices, were his pride and joy. That she was obviously in awe pleased him immensely. Being a decorator and in the luxury real estate business, she'd seen her share of high-end properties and had furbished many herself. Her opinion mattered and not just because she knew the industry and could spot quality and outside-the-box thinking. Beck wanted her to like his loft.

She stopped by the window and turned to face him. "I love this loft. Linc prefers a more traditional look for his listings and the décor I do for him." She gazed longingly at the brick wall, then glanced around the room again and sighed.

He debated whether or not to bring up the memory she'd triggered for him and decided what the hell. She obviously had strong feelings about her life she needed to face. "Last night you mentioned you were stuck in a boring job because your brother wouldn't let you branch out?" He stood her suitcase beside the hallway leading to the bedrooms and joined her by the window.

"I said that?" She wrinkled her nose in an adorable way.

He nodded. "You did. While you sat on the bed and cried."

She winced. "I remember that now. Look, I'm sorry I lost it on you. I–"

He shook his head and placed a hand beneath her chin, forcing her to meet his gaze. "Don't apologize. Why don't you explain what you meant?"

She raised her hands and dropped them to her sides before striding over to the sofa and sitting down. "So don't get me wrong. I love my brother–"

"So you've said," he muttered through gritted teeth. Just hearing Linc's name set him on edge.

Chloe shot him a curious look. "But our styles are completely different," she said without pressing him about her brother. "He likes conservative, safe designs, and just once I want to try stylish, fun trends on a rental or model and see what happens. He never lets me take a chance."

Sounded like Linc to him. When they'd been friends in college, he'd never been one to break the rules or push boundaries. Until that one night, that is. Beck clenched his fists and focused on Chloe.

"Take this place, for example. It's fantastic." She waved a hand around the room. "And it's not that I don't understand the concept of low risk that Linc likes to apply to business. I do. And what did playing it safe get me? I was left at the altar."

She nibbled on her bottom lip before continuing. "What if Linc let me take a step outside the box? But no, go with what's been selling, keep it within budget, and take efficiency into account," she said, mimicking her brother, and Beck did his best not to laugh.

She crossed one leg over the other, drawing his attention to the sexy-as-fuck boots she wore that came up high on her legs and had a small heel. Not to mention the body-hugging outfit that showed off her curves and had had him drooling from the moment she'd stepped out of the hotel bedroom.

Clearing his throat, he said, "I'm sure it's difficult to work for family or anyone who doesn't agree with your vision." He walked across the room, sat down beside her, placing a hand on her knee. "Sometimes you have to reach for what you want. Go out, grab the world by the balls, and go after it."

She met his gaze, those blue eyes focused on him. "What if you're afraid?"

He shrugged. "All the more reason to do it."

She pulled her bottom lip between her teeth and released it again, making him think about it being his mouth pressed to hers, his teeth taking that bite. Their bodies coming together in a clash of…

"So … show me to my room?" she asked.

He shook his head hard, reminding himself he should not be thinking about fucking his new roommate. And she clearly didn't want to talk about taking chances, so it was time to act like a good host.

He rose and extended his hand. She placed her palm in his, and damned if electricity didn't spark between them as he pulled her to her feet. "Come on."

"Wait." Her gaze was on their hands. "You suggested I put this somewhere safe." She pulled her hand out of his and eased the engagement ring off her finger. "I assume you have a safe in this apartment?"

He nodded and accepted the heavy ring in his hand. "Are you sure you trust me with it?" he asked, trying to lighten the moment.

And the way she rolled her eyes and grinned, he knew he'd accomplished his goal. He curled his hand around the ring, which he'd put in the safe in his bedroom until she was ready to deal with it.

"Bedroom's this way," he said, tilting his head. He led her to the spare guest room, grabbing her suitcase on the way.

His cell buzzed from his pocket. He ignored the call for now, guiding her down the hall and into the room across from his.

Something he hadn't given thought to until now.

The most gorgeous woman he'd ever laid eyes on, his ex-best friend's sister, and someone who needed his friendship more than anything else, was now living with him.

Keeping his hands to himself while giving her the shoulder she needed to lean on would be a challenge when all he wanted was to sweep her off her feet and take her to bed.

★ ★ ★

BECK WALKED CHLOE into the room, set her suitcase on the bed so she could unpack, and excused himself to return a phone call, as if he couldn't get away from her fast enough. Whatever. She didn't have the strength to worry about another man's moods. She had her own emotional state and life to fix.

With a sigh, Chloe sat down on the bed and took in her surroundings. The room was large and pretty, with white crown moldings and a light linen color on the walls. Windows let in a good amount of sunlight, giving the space a cheery feel, and the chic ruched taupe-colored comforter set was gorgeous, as were the decorative accents, lamps, and ultramodern fixture hanging from the ceiling. All reminders of the direction she wanted her career to go in.

She shook off that thought and decided to tackle one thing at a time, starting with unpacking. She rose, unzipped her suitcase, and put away her undergarments first, falling in love with the gorgeous white oak chest of drawers with nickel-finished hardware.

She placed the sexy bra and panty sets she'd

bought for her honeymoon in the drawers, including the lingerie, and did her best to ignore the gut punch at the reminder of what might have been. Despite having realized that she and Owen were a mistake, she couldn't deny wanting the family life he would have given her.

After putting her toiletries in the private bathroom attached to the room, she went to deal with the clothes she'd hang in the closet … and realized all she had packed were Hawaii-appropriate items. Long sarong skirts, bikini bathing suits, sandals, and sundresses. Everything to remind her of being dumped and nothing helpful for living in New York in the spring.

All her clothes were in boxes at her mom's house, waiting for her to bring them to the place she'd planned to live with Owen. Thank God he'd signed the lease and not her. The rent wouldn't be her problem, but the lack of clothing was. She couldn't have those huge boxes sent to Beck's, and she definitely wasn't ready to go to her mom's and face her disappointment and worry.

She wasn't sure what to do as she zipped up her suitcase and placed it on the floor in the corner of the room. Her cell rang, and she picked it up from where she'd placed it on the nightstand.

Jordan's name flashed on the screen, and Chloe answered, happy to talk to someone who would be rational about her situation.

She pressed *accept*. "Hey!"

"Hi, Chloe. How are you?" Jordan asked.

Flopping back down onto the mattress, Chloe left her feet hanging off the side so as not to put her boots on the bedspread. "I'm feeling less hungover, so that's an improvement."

Jordan chuckled. "Glad to hear it. Your brother came home really pissed off, and considering I pushed him to let you stay and party last night, I've been steering clear."

Chloe winced. "As if he has a say in what I do? When is he going to start treating me like an adult?" she asked, frustrated. "Never mind, that's a rhetorical question. But I am sorry if you're taking the brunt of my decisions."

"Seriously? When can't I handle your brother? It's fine. He's just pissed you're with Beck. Their history is … complicated," Jordan said.

Chloe glanced at her French manicure and thought about what she knew about Linc and Beck's falling-out back in college. "I remember meeting him when we went up for parents' weekend, freshman year. They were best friends, but then I never heard about him again until I went into business with Linc and Beck was both his competitor and enemy number one."

"Mmm." Jordan let out the sound.

"I'll take that to mean you can't say more. I respect that. I guess I'll just ask if I need to be worried about Beck? He's giving me a place to find peace for a little while, and I need that." Chloe would never ask Jordan to betray Linc's trust, but she did need to know if the man who'd stepped in was using her in any way as Linc had insinuated.

"No. I don't believe you need to be concerned," Jordan said. "I don't know Beck, but when Linc came home and told me where you were, I did some digging and asking around with people in the business. Beck seems to be a decent guy. Intensely competitive but nothing that stands out as an issue. Beck and Linc's problem is a personal one."

Chloe closed her eyes and expelled a relieved breath. "Thank you."

"That said, I wouldn't let my guard down completely. It was an ugly situation between them, and no one really knows how he'll react. And that's all I can really say on the subject."

Curiouser and curiouser, Chloe thought before turning her attention back to her brother and his soon-to-be wife. "I'm glad Linc has you, Jordan. And I'm glad you two realized taking that next step into a real relationship means what you share will grow deeper."

"Thanks, Chlo. You take care, okay? And if you ever change your mind, you're more than welcome to stay with us," Jordan reminded her before they said their goodbyes.

Then, Chloe pulled out her laptop she'd packed to take with her and began to do some online shopping. She also made calls to a couple of personal stylists she knew in order to fill in her wardrobe while she was staying with Beck.

★ ★ ★

BECK WITHDREW TO his bedroom, leaving Chloe alone in her new accommodations across the hall. For a man who kept his emotions locked up tight, Chloe brought out the oddest feelings, and he wasn't talking about his attraction to her, either. Her vulnerability reminded him of his sister. Whitney had had a bright smile, a big laugh, and she'd just begun to see who she might become as a woman when cancer had hit, but she'd also been a fighter. And she hadn't gone down easily.

He walked to his bedside drawer, opened it, and pulled out a piece of paper he'd had laminated so nothing would ever destroy his tangible memory of her. The words *Bucket List* were handwritten across the top of the page. A list of things Whitney wanted to do once she'd kicked cancer's ass. And when it became clear that wouldn't happen, a list she made Beck promise he'd complete for her. So one of them would fully live. He hadn't been Whitney's twin, but they'd been close nonetheless.

And he'd completed most of them. A tandem jump at Skydive Arizona, in the heart of the Sonoran Desert, which taught him extreme sports were not his thing, a hot air balloon ride in Albuquerque, New Mexico, the ballooning capital of the world, which had been phenomenal, and surfing lessons in Kauai, Hawaii. He'd enjoyed that experience but decided he'd prefer to be on a yacht instead of *in* the water. There were more things on the list he'd accomplished, and at each, he'd felt like his sister was with him, sharing the moments.

Only two remained. Seeing the northern lights and getting married. Of those, checking out the aurora borealis would happen. He'd been debating between a trip to Alaska and Norway, depending on how much time he wanted to be away. But the last item on her list would remain undone. Getting married was not in Beck's future. After Whitney had died, he refused to let anyone close enough for him to feel that kind of shattering loss again.

The buzz of his cell shook him out of the past. He put the laminated paper back into the drawer and closed it again before answering his phone to one of his brothers.

"Drew, what's up?" he asked.

"Just calling to find out what ended up happening last night."

Beck laughed. "You're the one who had a bridesmaid all over him. I should be asking you that."

"But you picked up the *bride* and carried her out of the ballroom. Sounds much more exciting to me. Where'd you go?" Drew asked.

Beck cringed as he replied. "I took her to the bridal suite."

"Jesus fuck, Beck. Tell me you dumped her in bed and left her to sleep it off."

With a groan, he settled onto his king-size mattress. "Something like that."

"How about you explain?" An attorney, Drew was never one to let something go without getting an answer.

Beck slid an arm behind his head, stretched out, and told him how last night had gone down with Chloe, how he'd carried her upstairs and settled her in.

"Kingston? Chloe Kingston, Linc Kingston's younger sister? That's whose wedding we crashed last night? Carrie, the bridesmaid, was too drunk to talk much, and eventually she left and stumbled upstairs with her friend who was all over Tripp," Drew said. "But back to you. Tell me you tucked her in and left her alone."

"Wish I could." Staring up at the ceiling, Beck bit

the bullet. "I stayed with her – nothing happened – and this morning I had a scene with her douchebag brother before telling her she could stay at my place until she figures out what to do with her life."

Beck pulled the phone away from his ear while his brother listed all the stupid reasons why having Chloe here was a bad idea. It started with her being a Kingston and ended with her being twenty-five to Beck's age of thirty-two.

"First off, it's not like she's underage. Second, we're platonic..." Despite his raging hard-on when he thought about Chloe. "Third, she's nothing like her brother, and the fourth and final point, how the hell do you know how old she is? I had no idea."

"I've been Googling while we're talking. First thing that came up was her non-wedding and being dumped at the altar by her ex. The article in the society page that came up first mentioned her age. Now tell me how you know she's nothing like her brother and why you'd bring a Kingston into your life after what Linc did to you?" Drew finished, sounding concerned.

As the older brother, Drew had always been protective of his younger siblings, and though Beck appreciated his concern, he knew what he was doing. "I trust my instincts and you should, too."

After all the years that had passed since Linc's betrayal, Beck had come to accept that Linc had still been drunk the morning he'd found him in bed with Jenna. Over the ensuing time at school, Beck had also seen his ex-girlfriend in action with other guys and learned she was no saint.

Beck wasn't about to renew his friendship with Linc or play nice, but he wasn't as blinded by anger and hurt as he once was. He just wanted to keep him at a distance.

"I'm coming over," Drew said.

"No–"

But Drew had disconnected the call, and Beck braced for a visit soon, considering his brothers both lived in a building Beck owned that was nearby. No doubt Drew wanted to meet Chloe and judge her for himself. Beck didn't appreciate his sibling getting into his business, but that's how his family rolled.

Sure enough, not long after the call, Drew arrived with Tripp in tow. Chloe had been in her room for almost an hour, and instead of checking on her, he gave her the time and space she probably needed.

"Don't you two have something better to do than check up on me?" Beck asked as they stepped inside.

"Not when you do something stupid like let a woman you barely know move in," Tripp said.

"One whose last name is Kingston." Drew shut the door behind them.

"Did I hear my name?" Chloe walked into the entryway, coming in from the hall, and his brothers turned her way. "Or my last name, anyway."

Beck frowned and glared at his brothers. "Chloe, these are my brothers." Asshole One and Asshole Two, he thought. "Tripp and Drew. Guys, meet Chloe."

"Hi," she said, treating them to a wave and a smile.

"Hi," Tripp said. "We met last night."

Chloe blushed and Beck shot his brother an annoyed glance.

"Yes, umm, last night I wasn't at my best. I'm sure you put the whole story together by now. Or read it somewhere," she said beneath her breath.

"It's not your fault," Beck said, irritated with his siblings.

"What do you have to eat? I'm hungry." Drew headed for the kitchen and they all followed.

Chloe stood by the refrigerator. "I know I'm a guest, but I'd like to be useful and not take advantage of Beck's hospitality. Can I get you something to eat or drink?" she asked Drew. "Let's see what we have." She opened the door and glanced inside.

"Chloe doesn't have to serve you," Beck said.

"I don't mind." She turned to face him and he shook his head.

"My brothers can get their own food or drink, but they didn't come here to eat. Now that you've met my new houseguest, maybe you can head home?" Beck suggested.

Tripp stepped up beside Chloe and glanced into the fridge, pulling out a can of Diet Coke and popping the top. "Actually, I spoke to Mom and Dad this morning, and I wanted to fill you guys in. So when Drew said he was coming by, I wanted to join him."

Chloe glanced at each of them. "I'm going to go back to my room and give you all some privacy. I just came out to tell you that I ordered clothes to be delivered here later today. Everything in my suitcase is for a honeymoon." She folded her arms across her chest and her cheeks flushed pink. "It was nice to meet you both. Today. When I'm not drunk. Never mind." She spun on her heel and walked out fast.

"Well. I hope you're happy. You've embarrassed her." Beck scowled, knowing he was going to have to apologize to her later.

But Tripp had said he was here about their parents, and Beck's gut had been telling him something was wrong. "Now what's going on with Mom and Dad?" Beck asked, gesturing for them to follow him into the more comfortable family room.

They settled in and Drew spoke first. "Sorry I jumped to conclusions about Chloe. I just wanted to make sure this wasn't some kind of setup by her brother."

"You're paranoid," Beck muttered. "Chill out, be nice to her and you're forgiven." He glanced at Tripp. "Spill it."

Tripp leaned forward in his seat on the couch. "I called this morning and pushed them for answers because Drew was right. Dad does look like he lost weight, and he didn't eat much of his favorite meal."

Tripp was the doctor in the family. If he was worried, then Beck's concern was warranted. "So what did they say?" he asked, turning his hands into fists and gripping hard.

"Dad has a colonoscopy next week. They didn't want to say anything and worry us. The good news is he just started feeling crappy. He hasn't put anything off, so if they find something, it's probably early stages." He glanced at Drew, who nodded before pinning Beck with a steady stare. "You heard me, right?"

"Yeah. I heard you." Beck had a tendency to jump to worst-case scenarios when it came to health scares.

The summer before Whitney passed away, they'd spent a lot of time together making her never-ending lists. Tripp hadn't been able to handle it and hadn't spent the same kind of time with her that Beck had, while Drew had been volunteering at the public defender's office to boost his academic resume for his ultimate goal of law school. Leaving in the fall, less than a month after Whitney had died, hadn't been easy.

"Snap out of it," Tripp said. "We don't know anything, so don't go spiraling into all the horrible possibilities. Go with what we know, which is he's having a test next week. That's all."

Beck braced his hands on his thighs and rose to his feet. "You're right. And I'm fine." No need to tell them he was worried sick. They probably already knew and felt the same way.

They hung out and talked for another half an hour before saying their goodbyes. Waiting until he knew they were gone and on their way, Beck called his parents to gauge for himself what was going on and how his dad was doing.

★ ★ ★

CHLOE HADN'T MEANT to eavesdrop on Beck and his brothers earlier. Unable to take feeling confined to a bedroom, she'd headed back out to the main part of the loft when she'd heard their voices.

She hadn't caught much. Just their concern about Beck letting Chloe stay here. Because she was a Kingston. Once again, she was curious about Linc and Beck's history and wondered if, at some point, she'd be able to ask one of them about it. She didn't take his brother's concerns personally.

If she let a stranger move in with her, her siblings would hit the roof, and if one of them brought an unknown woman into their place to live, she'd freak out, too. She was just glad Beck had family he was close with, like she did. Who knew? Maybe at some point she'd get to know Tripp and Drew and even win them over. She had a ways to go considering her behavior last night, she thought, cringing at the reminder.

She pulled off her boots, settled on the bed, and thought back to their conversation earlier about taking chances. Leaning over, she picked up the handbag she'd placed on the floor beside the bed and pulled out a piece of paper she'd been walking around with for weeks. The deadline to enter a prestigious design contest was coming up soon, one she'd been debating on whether or not to compete in.

The winner of the Online Interior Design Professional's Contest would receive a contract with Elevate Designs, an innovative online site that combined hiring an online designer with a tactile experience for the homeowner, sending them a curated box of paint chips, spec cards, and color and fabric samples. They catered to higher-end clientele who lacked the time to meet in person or go to showrooms to look at items but who wanted to spend on luxury.

Elevate was nothing like a mass site that hired any

designer with a portfolio. Located in LA, they were looking to have a New York City office, and the winner would be the person in charge. The entire thing was a risk, and Chloe was not known to be a risk-taker. But she'd still been preparing as if she intended to jump in.

In her free time, she'd learned various software applications that would let her lay out rooms and designs and had spent heaven only knew how many hours working on concepts, because she couldn't use anything she'd designed for Linc's business. Not with how conservative and staid his tastes ran. She'd been creating online rooms with 3D planner software, along with interactive and virtual floor plan designs.

With her supplier contacts, she'd also be able to decorate in the modern way she'd been dying to do. She'd put off having fabric and material samples sent to her until after her honeymoon. Since that wouldn't be happening, she emailed and arranged to have everything sent here. Although she would include images, she still needed to touch and feel the quality of materials for herself.

But entering meant stepping out of her comfort zone. If she won, and that was a long shot, it meant leaving the security of her job with Linc. And despite being frustrated with his safe way of doing things, she understood why he chose that direction. After all, hadn't she done the same thing by staying in her unfulfilling job and choosing her safe, or so she'd thought, ex-fiancé?

The slam of the apartment door jarred her out of her musings, and the muffled voices she'd heard earlier were gone. Beck's brothers had probably left. She gave Beck some more alone time before deciding it was okay to head back to the family room.

She found him staring out one of the windows, hands in his front pants pockets. Viewing him from behind was a treat. Broad shoulders and obvious muscles bunched on his upper arms and back, his rolled-up sleeves revealed tanned skin, and though his shirt was still untucked, she had a view of his ass and the back of his strong thighs in those dark jeans.

She didn't think she'd ever stopped to study Owen this way and knew, if she had, she'd have found him lacking in comparison.

Shaking off thoughts of her ex-fiancé, she cleared her throat to announce her presence. "Hi. Am I interrupting?"

He turned to face her. "No. I was just thinking."

His brother had come to talk about his parents, but from the closed-off look on his face, she decided not to ask any personal questions.

"Your brothers left?" she asked.

He nodded. "And I wanted to apologize. They can

be assholes."

She laughed at that. "I have three of them, remember? I know. And there's nothing to apologize for. They were just looking out for you. I mean, we just met last night. At least officially. I kind of remember you from the time my parents and I visited Linc in college."

He narrowed his gaze. "How old were you? Ten?"

"Eleven. But I'm twenty-five now." Like her brother, he was thirty-two. Seven years apart. Not that it mattered. There was nothing going on between them. "Is everything okay with your brothers?" She figured that was a simple enough question.

"They're fine but my father's going for a test sometime next week. He's lost some weight and we're all worried about him." Beck's jaw clenched tight, and she realized how badly this was affecting him.

Walking over, she put a hand on his forearm, her fingers coming into contact with warm flesh. "If there's anything I can do, please let me know."

"Thanks," he said in a gruff voice. "Are you all settled in?" he asked, changing the subject.

She nodded. "Except for the clothing situation, but I have personal shoppers who will be sending things over this afternoon so I'll be set for a while. All my stuff is boxed up at my mother's, and it was just simpler to handle it this way."

"Do you have a plan? I know you said you're taking this week off from work. To do what?" he asked.

"I was just thinking about that," she murmured, not quite ready to share her dreams and fears with anyone. "And I'm unsure."

He nodded. "Then let's tackle something simpler. How about dinner? Want to go out or order in?"

She knew the answer without having to think. "Order in. I'm not ready to face the world." She'd seen the gossipy mentions of her situation online and hated it.

"You got it, princess."

She liked the nickname he'd given her, not for the name itself but the fact that he was using one.

They agreed on Chinese food, and her clothing came while they were waiting for the delivery. She hung everything in her closet, planning to try things on and get back to the stylist in the morning. At least now she had seasonal clothing to wear.

She joined Beck in the kitchen, and they shared a meal of delicious General Tso's chicken, fried rice, pork dumplings, and she had an egg roll, her favorite part of any Chinese dinner.

Feeling full, she turned to him. "Are you finished?"

He nodded. "Totally full." He grabbed his plate and she shook her head.

"I've got it. I need to earn my keep," she said, only

partly joking, as she rose to her feet.

His frown was as sexy as his smile. "I offered you a place to stay. You don't have to earn anything."

"Well, then just let me help." She picked up his plate and hers and walked over to the sink.

After rinsing them off and putting everything in the dishwasher, she turned to find him placing the leftovers in the fridge. One container was still left on the table.

She grabbed it and came up behind him. "Here's the last one." Reaching around him, she placed the box on a shelf at the same time he turned her way, bumping into her.

His hand snaked out and grasped her waist, and they were face-to-face, their bodies in close contact. Heat erupted between them despite the chill of the refrigerator.

Her lips parted and she said the first thing that came to mind. "Thank you for being here for me." Which sounded much better than *Oh my God, you're so hot.*

He raised his hand, brushed her hair off her face, and cupped her cheek. "You're welcome."

She lifted onto her toes, intending to press her lips to his jaw. A little thank-you. Instead he turned his head and her lips met his.

She hadn't meant to kiss him, but with the firm

touch of his mouth on hers, she couldn't bring herself to move away. Neither did he, and what began as an accident quickly accelerated into something more. Something intense, unexpected, and wholly new, and at the touch of their tongues, sparks ignited.

Beck's hand came to rest on the back of her neck, gripping her possessively and holding her in place while he kissed her for all he was worth. Enjoying every moment, she slid her hands through his hair and pressed herself against his hard body.

He groaned and delved deeper into her mouth. She wasn't sure how long they stood entangled in each other, but she was aware of two things. She'd never been kissed like this before, and she wanted more. More of the rising desire inside her and more of Beck.

Without warning, he braced his hands on her shoulders and broke their connection. "Chloe, no. This is wrong."

She blinked in surprise. Cold, refrigerated air replaced his warmth, and the recognition of another rejection rushed through her. "You're right. This was a mistake." Wrapping her arms around herself, she stepped back.

He followed and closed the refrigerator door, obviously taking a moment before turning back to face her. It hadn't been enough time for her to pull herself together and fake being unaffected by his brush-off. It didn't matter. Considering she'd not only instigated the kiss but was a guest in his home, she owed him an apology.

"I'm sorry. I shouldn't have kissed you. I only meant it as a thank-you, but you turned your head and..." She trailed off, not wanting to rehash her embarrassment. "You've been kind, and if I made things awkward and you want me to leave, just say so."

"You're not going anywhere," he said in a gruff tone. "And you have nothing to apologize for because that kiss wasn't a mistake." His green-eyed gaze met hers, and it was anything but disinterested or dispassionate.

"Then why did you say it was wrong?" She cocked her head to one side, waiting for him to explain.

"That's easy. Because when we sleep together, and we *will*, it won't be because you're grateful or on the rebound. It will be because you can't think of anyone but me." His heated stare raked over her, his desire for her unmistakable, before he turned and walked out of the room, leaving her stunned. And more than a little bit turned on.

Chapter Four

A WEEK HAD passed since Chloe moved in with Beck. A week during which she'd given herself permission to grieve – not Owen but the life she'd thought she'd be living. Yes, a part of her wanted marriage and children with the right man, and she'd thought she'd been taking her first step in that direction.

Instead she was forced to confront her choices, and she wasn't happy with what she saw. A woman who'd graduated from college with a major in interior design but who'd taken the easy route, going into the family business and listening to her brother's dictates on layout, color schemes, and style. A woman who did as her family expected. One who chose a man because he was unlike her father in his moral compass, or so she'd thought, not because she was madly in love with him.

When she looked back, she realized Owen had talked her into the engagement, using all the buzzwords he knew would entice her, from them being a good fit to their wanting the same things to the fact that her parents approved. And when her father had been diagnosed with dementia, she'd fallen back into the pattern of a girl wanting to make her dad happy. She'd been holding on to the ideal of a parent who loved his family but lacked the ability to be faithful. But her brothers hadn't liked Owen, and that should have been her major clue.

She just hadn't wanted to hear it. Basically she'd been dancing to everyone's beat but her own.

She hopped off the bed and picked up the box with the samples that had been delivered midweek. Having already looked them over, she knew she'd chosen well. From tile to paint and everything else, she'd touched, ensured they were perfect.

Screw it, she thought, grabbing her laptop and pulling up the entry form for the contest that was already filled out and saved. She just needed to hit send, pay the fee, and when she was ready, forward her submission.

It was time she stood on her own two feet, but that didn't mean she wasn't nervous and scared about taking that step away from her family. She was well aware of how sheltered she'd been and wanted that to change. But, though she knew what she had to do, she wasn't about to share the news with anyone. If she failed and didn't final, let alone win, nobody had to know but her.

Drawing a deep breath, she filled in the credit card form and hit the enter button, then forced a calming breath as it processed. Finally the acceptance page appeared on the screen. There. She'd done it.

Step one toward independence.

★ ★ ★

BECK WALKED INTO the building where his office was located. Normally the sight of the property he owned, this place in particular, gave him immense pleasure. The 1930s hotel-like feel, with its black-steel-framed windows, the brushed brass fixtures, and glamorous décor let him swell with well-earned pride. Coming from a background where money was tight, he'd worked his way here and never let himself forget it.

Today, not even the reminder of success gave him the peace he needed. He sat at his desk, distracted for multiple reasons. His father's colonoscopy was at nine a.m., and his mother wouldn't let Beck or his brothers sit with her while she waited. She insisted everything was fine, the procedure was routine, and she'd be home with his dad in no time.

So he had to wait for her phone call, which left him at loose ends and with time on his hands. He couldn't concentrate on work, and that let him think about his houseguest.

Beck had been living under the same roof as Chloe

Kingston for a little over one week. She was an easy houseguest, careful to clean up not just after herself but him, wanting to make herself useful and show her gratitude. She didn't act like a spoiled princess despite his nickname for her, which had stuck. But as easy as she was to have around, that was as hard as she was to forget.

He was constantly aware of her. Cooking in his kitchen and sharing meals, curled up on the sofa in the family room, reading on an iPad or staring at the screen as if she had a lot on her mind, and sleeping across the hall from him. Her light cinnamon scent lingered everywhere she went, keeping him in a perpetual state of arousal. Especially after that kiss.

The memory of her sweet mouth had kept him hard as a rock and wide awake, knowing he'd turned her away. Ending things before they went further had been the right thing to do. Telling her they'd sleep together eventually hadn't been. And if he needed proof of why, the development project specs that came in his email from the architect he was working with reminded him.

Beck had made the deal with Kenneth Kingston, Linc and Chloe's father, who'd passed away a couple of months ago. He'd come to Beck with the proposal on the land deal and offered a piece of Kingston Enterprises as collateral if he couldn't come up with the payment for closing. Kenneth had died before that time came, and Linc had been in the dark about his dad's dealings.

On finding out, Linc had exploded, and Beck would be lying if he said he hadn't made it extra hard for his nemesis in the process. Linc had come up with the money, and not wanting anything to do with him, he'd left Beck to handle the deal.

Beck had only recently heard that Kenneth Kingston had been suffering from dementia and hadn't been of sound mind when making deals in his last couple of months. No wonder Linc had been pissed, and Beck didn't blame him for keeping the information to himself. To make it public would jeopardize the Kingston empire.

Clearly Chloe didn't know anything about Linc and Beck's dealings, personal or business. Getting involved with her would cause all sorts of drama in her life at a time when she needed her family. Besides, Chloe, the jilted bride, was a woman who intended to settle down, and Beck was a man intent on living his life without attachment. No attachment, no possibility of more loss.

This morning, he'd left Chloe asleep or so he assumed, considering he hadn't seen her before walking out the door. She was definitely falling into a state of, if not depression then definite moodiness, and needed someone to give her a kick and get her moving again in whatever direction made her happy.

So far she hadn't confided much about her life except for her frustration working within the confines of Linc's design needs. That didn't give him much to go on in how to help her.

Each night over dinner, he'd ask prodding questions about how she spent her day, and she'd always avoided a specific answer.

His cell rang. His brother's name flashed on the screen, and Beck answered immediately. "Tripp. Any news about Dad?"

"Nothing yet but it's early. I doubt they've even taken him in yet. Relax."

Beck released a ragged breath. "Okay, yeah. What's up?"

"One of my nurses had her Page Six app open, and guess what she was reading about? Your jilted bride," Tripp said before Beck could answer.

He closed his eyes and groaned. "Shit. The woman can't catch a break." It had been a week since her non-wedding, as she liked to call it. "Why are they still focusing on her?"

"Because her fiancé has been out with another woman, and he hasn't skimped on the PDA. People are wondering where the jilted bride has gone," Tripp said.

"Because she hasn't left my apartment," Beck muttered.

"Exactly. Look, I have a patient to see. I have to go. Whoever hears from Mom first, call the others. Talk to you soon." Tripp disconnected the call.

Knowing he wouldn't get anything done here, Beck decided to go home and wait for the call from his parents. He walked out of his office, pausing by his assistant's desk.

"I'm leaving for the day. Cancel my afternoon appointment. Call me for emergencies only," he said to Ronnie.

"Yes, Mr. Daniels." She looked up from her computer and smiled.

"Thanks." He headed toward the elevator when he heard his name and turned to see Natasha Banks, a family friend since childhood and now his in-house designer for Beck Realty, walking toward him, iPad in hand.

Natasha had been close friends with Tripp and Whitney when they were younger and had remained close with them all ever since.

"Beck. Where are you going so early?"

"Home to wait on word about my father. He's having a procedure done and I'm useless here."

"Oh, I'm sorry." Reaching out, she placed a hand on his shoulder. "Is there anything I can do? Would you like some company?"

"No, thanks. I just need to be alone." Except he wouldn't be by himself. Chloe would be at his apartment. And suddenly being with someone else while he paced didn't seem so bad.

"Okay, well… I'll check in on you later." She squeezed his shoulder and smiled. "Send your dad my best."

"I will." He strode over to the elevator and headed home, where a blue-eyed beauty waited for him.

★ ★ ★

CHLOE SAT ACROSS from her newfound sister, Aurora, and her adorable baby daughter, Leah, who was about ten weeks old. When Aurora had called and asked if she could come visit, Chloe had immediately agreed. She didn't think Beck would mind her having someone over, and Aurora was worried after the mess of Chloe's non-wedding the week before. She admitted to herself she'd been hiding out at Beck's, but she wasn't any closer to deciding her next step.

She and Aurora had spent the morning talking, and Chloe had shown her the clothes she'd had sent over, keeping the mood light. She didn't want her family any more concerned about her than they already were, so she deliberately hadn't given Aurora anything concerning to report back to her brothers or mother.

"I love your new clothes," Aurora said. "I can't wait to lose the baby weight and be able to get nice clothes that fit." Aurora patted Leah on the back until the infant gave a burp that would make any of their brothers proud. Aurora laughed. "She's a pro at that."

Chloe grinned. "Give her to me." She gently accepted the baby, cuddling her in her arms and breathing in the delicious scent of her shampoo. "Mmm. You're a sweet girl," she cooed into the infant's ear.

"That's because she's not keeping you up all night screaming," Aurora said wryly. She pulled her long blond hair into a ponytail and yawned.

"Do you want to take a nap in my room? I can watch her for a little while," Chloe offered.

Aurora shook her head. "I'll nap when I get back home. Your mom said she'd take her for a little while this afternoon."

Her mother was a saint, taking a pregnant Aurora into her house and giving her a home and family. A saint because Aurora was her husband's illegitimate child.

"Mom loves Leah," Chloe murmured. Melly, her mother, treated Leah like she was her first grandchild and Aurora as if she were her daughter.

Everyone in the family wanted to give them a soft place to fall because Aurora's life had been hard. She'd just turned nineteen last week, and Chloe didn't know how Aurora had managed to get by prior to Linc finding out about her and traveling to Florida to meet and bring her home.

"Why won't you come back to the house?" Aurora asked. "Your mother wants you to stay there, and I'd love to have you around."

"You'd love an extra set of hands for the baby, you mean?" Chloe laughed.

Aurora rolled her eyes. "It *would* help but that's not what I meant."

"I know and I appreciate you wanting me there." Getting to know Aurora had been wonderful these past months.

Aurora shifted in her seat. "Linc isn't happy you're here." She swept her arm around, indicating Beck's apartment. "He says it's because you don't know Beck at all and you belong with family."

Chloe sighed. "Please tell Linc I'm staying with Beck because he's not family, and he won't try and strong-arm me into decisions I'm not ready to make. I know he loves me but I'm fine here. I have time and space to think about what I want to do with my life … without anyone pressuring me."

"I will. But what do you mean you need to think about what you want to do with your life?" Aurora wrinkled her nose in confusion. "You already have a job. You just need a place to live."

"I guess this sudden change has shaken me out of my comfort zone. I'm not getting married, and it's forcing me to reevaluate what I need to make me happy. Can we leave it at that?"

Chloe bit down on the inside of her cheek. Lying didn't come naturally to her, but she didn't want to put Aurora in an uncomfortable position by telling her she was unhappy in her job with Linc, nor did she want anyone to know about the contest she'd entered and the possibility of a new career if she won. Whatever changes Chloe decided to ultimately make, she had to face her brother on her own.

"Sure. I can understand that."

The sound of the door opening was followed by footsteps as Beck strode into the room where they were sitting. "I see we have company."

His gruff voice sent tremors of awareness rushing through Chloe's veins. Baby in her arms, Chloe rose to her feet. "Beck, this is my sister, Aurora. Aurora, meet Beck Daniels, the guy who graciously took me in."

At the sight of him, Aurora's eyes opened wide, and Chloe couldn't blame her. The man was always an exceptional example of the male species.

Today, though, he appeared distracted and disheveled. His long hair looked like he'd been running his fingers through the strands, and though dressed for work in a pair of black jeans that hugged his firm thighs and a dress shirt rolled at the sleeves and unbuttoned, showing his tanned chest, his entire appearance was *off*. She hadn't known him for long, but the look in his eyes also spoke volumes, making her wonder what was bothering him.

Aurora stood and extended her hand, shaking Beck's. "It's nice to meet you. And I can see now why Chloe would rather stay here. With you." Glancing at Chloe, Aurora grinned.

Chloe closed her eyes and groaned. She'd forgotten how easily thoughts slipped from Aurora's brain straight out of her mouth. Somehow she'd been living with the man and had pushed their kiss to the back of her mind. Otherwise she'd be shifting between being eternally mortified and always aroused at the thought of *when* they slept together. Because he'd made it clear the time would come.

But she didn't need Aurora stoking a banked flame. She shot her sister a warning glare, but Aurora merely shrugged. "What? I'm just calling it like I see it."

Beck let out a laugh, and even that reverberation from deep in his chest was sexy.

"It's nice to meet you, Aurora. I needed a good laugh this morning, so thank you," Beck said.

Aurora treated Chloe to a pleased smile. "I think

it's time to take Leah home. Now that she's fed, she'll sleep the whole car ride and be wide awake when we get back. Just in time for your mother to take over."

"You make sure you get some sleep while Mom's got her," Chloe said, handing Leah back to her mother.

Aurora packed up her baby bag and let the driver know she was ready to leave. Because Aurora hadn't yet learned to drive, Linc had insisted she have a driver at her disposal so the baby would be safe in a car seat as opposed to using a ride share app.

Chloe shook her head, wondering how the younger girl was really handling all these life changes. She'd have pushed for answers, but who was she to question when she didn't want to answer things for herself?

Aurora said her goodbyes and headed out to the elevator.

Chloe waited until the door closed and walked back into the apartment, finding Beck still in the family room.

He stood by the window, hands in his pockets, staring out at the view. She strode up and joined him, looking out in silence. If he had something to say or share, she hoped he'd trust her enough to do it.

Just when she'd almost given up, he forced out a heavy groan. "My father has a procedure this morning. A colonoscopy and I'm waiting to hear how he made out. I couldn't focus on work, so I came home."

Hmm. "Isn't that normally a routine test?" she asked, hoping that's all it was for Beck's dad.

He shifted on his feet and turned to face her. "Yeah. But he looks like he's lost weight, and my parents were avoiding the subject until they had no choice but to tell us." When he dipped his head, she could almost feel the weight on his shoulders.

"When are you supposed to hear something?" she asked.

He glanced at his gold Rolex. "Soon." His shoulders were stiff, and she had the sense there was much more to the story than what he was telling her.

"How about I make some coffee and we can wait together?"

He met her gaze, gratitude in his green eyes. "I'd like that."

A few minutes later, they were settled in the kitchen, sitting on the barstools at the counter, coffee mugs in hand.

"So distract me," Beck said. "When I was in school with Linc, you were the youngest Kingston sibling. How did Aurora come to be family?"

Chloe took a sip of her hot drink. "Well, that's a complicated story. After my father passed away a couple of months ago, Linc found a pile of cashed checks in his desk. Monthly checks from a bank account no one knew about written to a woman who'd been his secretary almost twenty years ago. Linc did some tracing and uncovered one of Dad's dirty secrets."

"He'd had an affair?" Beck easily guessed.

She nodded. "One of many, but after following the trail, it led to finding out we had a sister. To make a very sad story short, my father had gotten Aurora's mother pregnant. When she refused to have an abortion, he paid her to stay away and raise the baby on her own." Chloe shivered at the callousness of her dad's actions. It still galled her.

"So Linc found Aurora and her mother when he went looking?" Beck asked, hand under his chin, clearly interested in the story.

Chloe wrapped her hands around the mug and shook her head. "He found Aurora. Suffice it to say my father paid her mother to live a fun lifestyle while she left her daughter in foster care. And before you ask, yes, my father knew and left her there, too." Her throat swelled as she told the bare basics of her sister's story, which was so sad it broke Chloe's heart.

As if he understood, Beck reached out and squeezed her hand. "I'm sorry."

The warmth of his touch sizzled through her, and it was all she could do not to lean into him. "Thank you." She managed a smile. "But when Linc found out about her, he did everything he could to find her and convince her to come to New York with him. And when he finally tracked her down, he discovered a very pregnant young girl." Chloe shrugged. "And here we are."

Beck let out a low whistle. "She's lucky Linc found her."

"At the time, she'd just started to get her life together, but we're all happy she decided to come to New York and get to know us," she said.

He smiled. "I could tell how you felt when I saw you two together." He drummed his fingers on the counter and lines appeared on his forehead, letting her know his mind was drifting back to worry about his own family.

Before she could come up with another topic of conversation, he spoke. "So what else have you been doing to keep busy while I'm at work? Have you gotten out of the house at all?"

She forced a smile. Like Aurora, she didn't want Beck to be concerned about her, so she placated him the best she could. "I'm keeping busy," she said vaguely, and when she caught the disappointed look in his eyes, she knew she had to elaborate. She just wouldn't include telling him about her contest entry.

"I did the same things as usual. I watched television, read a book, and checked out social media, ignoring the gossip sites. And no, I didn't go out. There's nothing I really need right now."

She hated being part of a family that generated interest, but wealth tended to do that. Although Linc and Jordan's engagement had hit the media, her pregnancy was still under wraps, and they planned on an intimate ceremony soon. They hadn't wanted to upstage Chloe's wedding by marrying quickly.

"I get ignoring the gossip shit. Nobody deserves to be put under a microscope." He glanced away then asked, "Are you okay? About what happened with the wedding?" It was the first time he'd asked her about her emotional state, and she couldn't help but be honest.

She ran her finger around the rim of her mug. "I'm sad about losing the life I thought I wanted. I'm not upset about Owen. I'm better off without him."

He grinned. "Glad to hear it. That's an important distinction to make. It'll help you heal quicker."

She nodded.

"What about going back to work for Linc? Wasn't your honeymoon a week?" he asked.

"Two weeks. Nobody expects me back yet." And now that she'd entered the contest, she wanted to perfect her submission.

"Aren't you getting bored at home?" He took a drink of his coffee, and her gaze was drawn to his soft-looking lips. Lips that had kissed her with talent and expertise, arousing her beyond belief.

"Chloe?" he asked.

Caught staring and knowing what she'd been remembering, she shook her head and hoped she wasn't blushing. "I'm fine. Taking some rest and relaxation is good for me. Just like a honeymoon, huh?"

The ring of Beck's phone interrupted any possible reply.

Shooting her an apologetic glance, he answered, obviously eager. "Mom. What's going on?"

Chloe gripped her mug tight as he listened to whatever his mom had to say, praying for good news. She couldn't decipher much from the grunts and uh-uhs she heard.

"Okay, Mom. I get it. I love you and tell Dad the same. I'll check in later." He listened some more and then said, "I'm fine. I swear. I'll talk to you soon." He disconnected the call and met Chloe's gaze, his own expression somber.

"Well?"

He expelled a deep breath of air. "They found some polyps and sent them out for biopsies. We have to wait for answers."

She nodded. "Okay, so no news is good news, right?"

Jaw set, he shrugged. "I guess we'll see. I've

learned not to trust what a doctor promises. You never know what will happen."

She narrowed her gaze, wondering what had made him so wary and distrustful of the profession. "Isn't your brother a pediatrician?" Beck had mentioned it sometime this past week.

He nodded.

"I know it's not the same thing, but why don't you see how he feels about the news?" She hated seeing him so upset.

"Thanks for trying to help. I think I'm just going to change and head to the gym to work out. I'll feel better after I beat on something."

She watched him go, worried about how withdrawn he'd suddenly become.

★ ★ ★

A COUPLE OF days passed during which Beck waited and angsted over getting his father's results. Everyone tried not to talk about it, but the shadow hovered over everything Beck felt and did. He spent a lot of time in the gym, punching a bag, trying to relieve his frustration that cancer could be something his family had to deal with again. At the thought, the old fear over what that meant rose inside him again.

Back at the apartment, he often caught a worried look on Chloe's face as she stared at him, sensing his distress. Why didn't he just tell her he'd lost his sister to cancer, the same disease he feared losing his father to? Because he hated talking about it. When he thought or spoke about the past, the pain came back as if it were new and just as raw.

He'd rather focus on other things he could control, and after another few days of Chloe's moping around the house, he intended to do just that. He hoped Linc liked surprises, because he was about to get a big one.

Beck had never seen the need for a driver and took an Uber uptown to Kingston Enterprises. He approached the main desk, gave his name and ID, and after a quick phone call, was directed upstairs to Linc's floor.

A receptionist led him through the office, decorated just as Chloe had said, in a staid navy and taupe, looking like many other places he'd seen. No wonder Chloe was bursting to branch out. The vibrant woman he'd seen the night of her wedding and the morning after was slowly wilting the longer she remained holed up in his apartment. And she wouldn't get any better if she remained working with Linc.

But first things first. He needed to prod her out of being down in the dumps. She obviously had no real plan for the future, and he figured she needed the very people she was avoiding more than she wanted to admit.

He approached a desk, where Linc's fiancée and personal assistant sat guarding his office.

Catching sight of him, Jordan rose to her feet. "I have to admit I was surprised when the guard downstairs called and said you were here to see Linc."

"So was I." Linc, dressed in his ever-present suit and tie, stood in the doorway. "But considering my sister is staying with you, I'm guessing we have something to talk about. Come in." He glanced at Jordan. "Why don't you join us. You're just going to listen in anyway," he said with a grin Beck knew he reserved for very few. "I take it you don't mind."

"Not at all," Beck said. It hadn't been a question anyway.

Beck gestured for Jordan to precede him, and they all walked into Linc's office. Jordan took a chair. Linc leaned against his desk, arms folded in front of him.

And Beck stood in front of him. "Well, this is cozy."

"Cut the crap," Linc muttered. "What brings you here? Is Chloe okay?"

"Yeah," Beck answered immediately because he wouldn't let Linc think anything was wrong with his sister. "But she's not herself. I'm not sure I'd say she's depressed, but she's down for sure."

Linc stiffened. "How can you be sure? You barely know her," he said through clenched teeth.

"Linc." Jordan rose and walked over to him, placing a hand on his shoulder. "Let him explain without biting his head off."

Beck flashed her an appreciative smile. "I know because Chloe hasn't left my apartment, and she doesn't seem to have motivation to do anything more. Even when Aurora came over, Chloe enjoyed herself, but she definitely didn't think about going out while she was there. Maybe because they had the baby, I don't know. But I thought you should know."

Linc nodded, taking in Beck's words. "She needs her family, which is what I said from the minute that bastard left her at the altar," he muttered.

"But she's an adult and made her choice to stay with me. I'm just giving you the courtesy of letting you know how she's doing. In person."

A long pause followed, and Beck thought Jordan was going to have to nudge Linc to get a thanks, but he managed to speak up first.

"Thank you," he finally said.

"I'm doing it for Chloe." Beck needed to make his position clear.

"We'll take care of her," Jordan said and Beck had no doubt she meant it. Linc, too.

Like Beck and his family, the Kingstons were a tight bunch.

His job here finished, Beck turned and walked out of the office, heading back downtown to his loft. That Chloe was there waiting made it all that much sweeter.

Chapter Five

OTHER THAN AURORA'S visit, Chloe had managed to hold her family off for over a solid week. And if it had been Linc who'd called asking her to meet, she could have pushed him for more time, too. Not Xander. Her marine turned thriller writer brother liked his solitary lifestyle, staying in his East Hampton home whenever he could and only coming to his Manhattan apartment when necessary.

If Xander was asking to see her, she couldn't say no. He suggested they meet at her mother's estate in Brookville, which was halfway for each of them, an hour for her and actually half an hour longer for him. Leaving Beck a note so he wouldn't wonder where she'd suddenly disappeared to when he returned from work, she called for an Uber and headed to her mom's.

As the car stopped at the gate, Chloe opened her window and punched in the code. The doors slowly opened, and the driver pulled up to the house she'd grown up in. Massive and with enough land for her father to dub it the Kingston Estate, this was home.

She thanked the man and exited the vehicle, immediately taking in not just Xander's BMW SUV but Linc's Range Rover and Dash's obscene Ferrari Limited Edition V12 supercar. Given his rock star status as lead singer of the Original Kings, to Dash, the sports car was pocket change. He had the kind of fame that put her little issue with social media bloggers and Page Six to shame. Surprise hit her that he was at their mother's, too. The band should be holed up writing music and practicing the songs they had ready so they could head off on tour. Instead Dash was here along with the entire family.

Which told Chloe one thing: She'd been set up.

Her anger bubbled up along with a deep understanding of their concern. After all, if the situation were reversed and any one of them had been left at the altar and taken refuge with a stranger, she'd be out of her mind with worry, as well. But that didn't mean they could manipulate her.

The front door was unlocked, and she let herself inside, following the sound of voices to the large family room her mother had redone shortly before Chloe's father had passed away of a heart attack.

She stood in the wide entry, taking in the busy-looking chintz furniture covered with floral fabric and accented with dark wood. All her mother's taste. Not Chloe's.

In silence, she waited until, one by one, they noticed her.

"Honey, I'm so glad you're home." Her mother walked up to her and pulled her into a hug, and Chloe doubted anyone had told her mom that this was an ambush.

"Hi, Mom." She hugged her back, taking in her familiar scent.

Breaking apart, she met Xander's gaze. "You," she said, pointing at her bearded brother, "used our relationship against me."

"Whoa." He held up both hands. "All I did was ask to see my sister. With a little prodding from him." Xander tilted his head toward Linc and Jordan groaned.

"Can't you keep your mouth shut?" Linc muttered.

"What? Because it isn't obvious that this gathering means it's time to have a *chat* with Chloe?" she asked with finger quotes around the word *chat*.

"I thought you all decided to come for a visit," her mother said, her chiding gaze falling from one male child to the next.

Linc stepped toward Chloe. "Well, now that you're here, can you at least understand that we're worried about you? Holed up in Beckett Daniels's place? You don't even know him." He reached out a hand to touch her arm and she jerked away.

Chloe dropped her shoulders and much of her anger. "Of course I understand you're concerned. I would be, too, if the situation was reversed. But the whole point of me staying with Beck is that he's not pressuring me. I have time to think and assess my life. When things get upended, that's what you do."

Dash, who'd been leaning against a far wall, stood straighter. "She deserves time to weigh her options and her life choices," he said, and she shot him a grateful look.

"By moping around? Not going out or leaving the apartment?" Linc asked. "I don't call that healthy behavior."

Chloe narrowed her gaze. "Just how did you know that?"

"I didn't say a word to anyone about anything! I swear. Except relaying your message to Linc," Aurora said, obviously afraid Chloe would think she'd mentioned something to cause this intervention after her visit.

"I know." Chloe softened her expression as she met her sister's gaze. "This isn't about anything you did." Unfortunately she had a feeling she knew who'd actually been behind this meeting.

And if Beck wanted her to leave, all he'd had to do was ask. He hadn't had to go behind her back to her brother, a man he didn't even like, to push her away.

Hurt rose up inside her. "What did Beck say?" she asked Linc, talking over the painful lump in her throat.

Jordan stepped forward and nudged Linc out of the way. "Go. You've done enough damage," she told him. "Chloe, look. All Beck said was that he was concerned that you're feeling down, and he thought maybe you could use a talk with your family."

Swallowing her sense of betrayal to deal with later, she nodded. "I appreciate that but nobody needs to worry about me. I have plans." She sought to reassure them.

"Like coming back to work?" Linc asked, sounding hopeful.

"Linc, stop being so pushy. She knows you care but you're going overboard." Her mom glanced at Chloe and gave her a warm smile. "And what *did* you decide, honey?"

Chloe rubbed her hands up and down her arms. She sighed, knowing there wasn't much she could do but confess, and turned to her oldest brother. "I haven't been happy with my job for a while."

"What? Since when?" Linc asked.

Chloe blinked, realizing how dense men could be. They didn't pick up obvious signals. "You know I've asked to branch out into more eclectic design in our more modern buildings. To be able to use my talents more. And you always shoot me down."

He frowned and didn't reply right away, which meant at least he was thinking about her feelings because Linc loved her. They all did, and since Beck had instigated this get together, Chloe could understand their renewed concern.

"I just believe in sticking to what works," he finally said.

Chloe sighed. "And I respect your business sense, but I need more to satisfy me." Drawing a deep breath, she said, "I entered the Elevate Online Interior Design Professional's Contest." Putting herself out there wasn't easy. Telling her family her intentions meant they would know if she failed and lost the contest. If so, she'd have to go crawling back to Linc with her tail between her legs, and that wasn't an easy thing to face.

Surprise lit his gaze while the rest of the family remained silent. She assumed most of them had no idea what the contest was all about, but Linc did. She'd shown him past years' winners only to have him shrug their designs off as *not the Kingston way.*

"What's the contest about?" Aurora asked.

Chloe knew this was the moment where she took that leap of faith by revealing her hopes and dreams. "It's a prominent interior design contest. This year the winner not only gets a contract with the company but they're looking for someone to run the New York branch they plan to open next year."

Linc stared in shock. "You're planning to leave the family business?"

She straightened her shoulders. "If I win, then yes."

Xander clapped his hands, supporting her. "Why not? I'm not part of Kingston Enterprises and neither is Dash." After striding over, he put an arm around Chloe's shoulders. "Neither is Aurora for that matter."

"But she has that option if she wants it." He shot a warm glance Aurora's way. "And as for you two, you have talents that took you elsewhere," he said about Xander and Dash.

"And I don't?" Chloe asked, hurt by his innuendo.

He shook his head. "I didn't mean it that way. It's just that…"

Chloe waved her hand through the air, cutting him off. "I know your intentions are good but right now you're not helping. You're only making things worse."

It was in Linc's nature to take charge, and she loved him for being like a parent when her own father never had been. But Chloe had reached the point where she wanted to live her own life, and she desperately needed Linc to understand. Everyone else seemed to.

She swept her gaze around the room. "I love you all and thank you for worrying. I promise if I need you, I'll call." Pulling out her phone, she engaged the Uber app and requested a car.

Walking out of the room, she left them talking behind her.

She stepped into the spring air, and knowing she had time, she sat down on the front step. Tears welled in her eyes while she waited for her ride.

Linc wanted everyone happy but under his umbrella and terms, and for years, she'd made it easy for him to think his way was the right one. Now, though, she'd taken that first step toward independence and was petrified about what would happen if she stumbled.

She heard the sound of the front door opening but didn't turn to see who was joining her.

"Hey." Xander lowered himself beside her, stretching out his long legs on the steps leading to the bluestone path.

"Hi." She rested her chin on her knees.

"You know Linc means well, right?" Xander asked.

She shot him a surprised glance. "You're defending him?"

Xander groaned. "We both know he's a little harsh in his delivery, but it's just because he loves you. He loves all of us. And he'll get used to you doing what's best for you, even if it's not what he wants. I promise."

She managed a smile. "I know. And I'm not really

mad at him or anyone in the family." Beck was another story.

He pulled her into a brotherly hug. "Personally I think you're going to kick ass in this contest, by the way."

"Thanks. You're a pretty decent big brother," she said with a laugh, resting her head on his shoulder.

"Look, I don't know this Beck Daniels, either, but I have that huge house in East Hampton or the usually empty apartment in the city. You can stay with me and have all the privacy you want or need."

And if she moved out of Beck's, she might take Xander up on his offer, something she'd decide after she had it out with her host. "Thanks. If I need you, I promise to let you know."

Of everyone in her family, Xander understood needing time and space the best. He had mild PTSD from his time in the marines and preferred the uncluttered Hamptons to the bustle of New York City. Everyone gave him the space he needed. Why couldn't they do the same for her?

They sat in silence until her car arrived and she headed home to deal with Beck.

★ ★ ★

CHLOE HAD AN hour-long ride back to the city to work up her anger and frustration with Beck. He should have come to her with his concern for her welfare or his desire to get rid of her as his roommate. She entered the apartment with the app he'd programmed on her phone and looked around the kitchen and the family room first, not finding the man she needed to talk to.

She stormed to her room, put down her purse, and kicked off her shoes, noticing on the way that Beck's door was closed. With the long day she'd had and all the travel and traffic, she was exhausted. She'd even had the driver stop at a fast-food place so she could grab something for dinner on her way home from her mom's. She'd figured she needed all the energy she could get for the confrontation to come. And she didn't plan on waiting until morning to have it.

She stepped out of her room and across the hall, knocking on Beck's bedroom door. "Beck, open up. We need to talk!" She banged again, her hand midair as the door flung open and Beck stood in front of her.

He grasped her wrist before her hand, already in motion, could hit him in the chest. "Whoa. What's wrong?"

She'd intended to rip into him for siccing her family on her, but she hadn't planned on the bare-chested man greeting her in gray sweats. Muscles defined his pecs and abs, biceps and triceps. Not to mention, everyone knew how much gray sweatpants revealed on a well-endowed man. Beck sported an extremely large bulge in his sweats, and at the sight of him, her mouth went dry.

"Chloe?" he asked as he released his grip, and she lowered her hand to her side.

Gathering herself, she straightened her shoulders and recalled the reason for her bedroom visit. "If you wanted me gone, all you had to do was say so. You didn't have to go to my family so they'd gang up on me in an attempt to get me to come home." Though to be fair, the only one who'd really pushed for that was Linc.

Beck narrowed his gaze. "That's not why I did it. You haven't left this apartment in over a week. You've admitted you're miserable in your job, and from where I stood, you had no solid plans for yourself going forward. A bright, beautiful woman like you deserved better, and given how close you are to your family, I figured they could help shake you out of the funk you've been in."

"Oh." Her mind homed in on the words *bright* and *beautiful*, and some of her anger ebbed.

"Yeah. *Oh*. And for the record, if I wanted you gone, I'd have the balls to tell you myself." He stepped back, one hand on the doorframe. "Come in and let's talk."

Suddenly she wanted to do more than talk. The

idea of getting up close with this man, all that bare, hot skin pressing against her, had her hot and bothered.

Overly aware of him, she stepped into his bedroom, taking in his personal space for the first time. An accent wood wall behind his king-size bed warmed up the room. Earthy tones worked to give it a masculine feel, with a television on the wall across from the bed. Despite the décor being tailored for a man, Chloe felt comfortable in here. Or she would if the bed wasn't rumpled and unmade, giving her already heated body dirty thoughts of what they could do between those sheets.

"Like what you see?" Arms folded across his chest, a sexy smirk lifted his lips as he'd obviously caught her staring at his bed.

"I love it," she said, leaving what she was referring to purposely vague.

He walked past her and sat down on the edge of the mattress, patting the space beside him.

She eased beside him, bending one leg, her knee brushing his hard thigh. "But seriously, you should have come to me with any concerns you had … about me."

He nodded. "You're right. I was thinking more about what your family could do for you than what was the right way to handle it. I'm sorry."

Her lips twitched at his apology. "You're forgiven." She paused. "You're still okay with me staying here?"

"I kind of like having you around." His eyes glittered with a sudden heat that matched the spark he ignited inside her.

"And I like being here."

He held her gaze and she caught the question in his eyes… Was this the right time for them?

★ ★ ★

THE PROVERBIAL DEVIL sat on one shoulder, urging Beck to splay Chloe out on his bed and make a feast of her sexy body. An angel sat on the other, reminding him she was just coming out of a relationship, was vulnerable, and if she were going to turn to a new man, it shouldn't be one who had issues with her family, or at least with one of the brothers she loved.

He wanted to help her, not complicate her life. But the thought of Chloe with any guy other than him brought out an inner caveman he hadn't known existed.

"You're overthinking. And I promise you I can make my own decisions." She braced her hands on the space between them and leaned forward. "I'm looking to let go and have some fun."

Her damp lips beckoned to him, but he wouldn't go into this with anything less than the truth between them. "I don't do relationships," he told her bluntly.

She lifted a delicate shoulder. "I just got out of one. I'm not looking to get tied down again either."

"What about the fact that you're the type of woman who has marriage stamped all over her?" And he'd promised himself not to add to the people in his life he could ultimately lose.

"And I didn't think you were the kind of man to stereotype me just because, when you met me, I was wearing a wedding dress."

She laughed at her own joke, and he couldn't help but grin as well. "What about our living arrangement?" he asked.

"This will only complicate things if we let it. How about we go with the flow?"

He raised an eyebrow, enjoying this sassy, confident side of her, so similar to the woman he'd met a short week and a half ago. And she was right. It was her choice.

She moved in, her lips hovering near his. Teasing. Tempting. His dick was hard as a rock, and all he had to do was roll her onto her back and take what she was offering.

And she *was* offering.

"Sounds like we're on the same page," he said, closing the distance and capturing her mouth with his.

This kiss wasn't soft and needy, it was rough and

full of desire and life, something he hadn't experienced with a woman … ever. With Chloe, it wasn't a scratch the itch and get over it, it was already more.

From the minute he'd laid eyes on her, even after he'd realized she was a Kingston, he'd felt protective. Nothing else explained his taking her to the bridal suite. Staying. Giving her a place to crash. Going to Linc on her behalf. If anyone was going to need to get on the same page and shore up walls, it was him. And he would.

After he took her to bed.

He lifted his mouth from hers, rose, and pulled her to her feet.

"What are you doing?" she asked.

"Undressing you so I can see you naked on my bed." His gruff voice took him by surprise.

And with that, he slid her cropped jacket off her shoulders, and she shimmied until it fell to the floor. Next he raised the hem of her camisole, and with her help, the silk went over her head and arms, joining the pile he'd started.

His gaze zeroed in on the sexy beige bra with lace on the edges of the cups, her nipples hard and visible through the flimsy material. Reaching out, he pinched one distended bud, twisting with his fingers until she shifted her hips and moaned.

Pleased at her reaction, he gave the other nipple

the same treatment, holding on as she gripped his shoulders and dug her nails into his skin. He liked that she showed her emotions, that she didn't hide her responses from him. Undoing the bra and slipping it off, he deposited it along with the rest of the clothing.

He raised his head and brushed a kiss over her lips before he undid the button on her low-cut jeans. Hooking his fingers into the waistband and grasping her panties along with them, he helped her wriggle out of them until finally she was naked.

He looked her over and expelled a harsh breath, his cock tenting his sweats, the rush of desire almost unbearable. Dropping to his knees, he grasped her hips in his hands and pressed butterfly kisses over the indentation along her belly where her panties had been. Arousal dripped from her sex, the scent telling him how much she wanted him. As much as his throbbing cock wished he'd give relief and thrust himself inside her.

She arched her hips, thrusting her sweet pussy forward. Without waiting, he parted her with his thumbs and swiped his tongue over her clit. Her legs shook and she gripped his shoulders again, this time her nails digging in harder, and he wouldn't be surprised if he had marks later.

He licked her everywhere, teasing her plump lips and nipping at her clit before soothing with longer wet laps of his tongue.

"Oh, God. More, Beck, please. I need so much more," she said, her body trembling and shaking. Her hips arched, and she raised herself onto her toes, grinding herself against his mouth.

He held on tight, not releasing her, not breaking contact, determined to bring her up and over the edge and give her the release she so obviously needed. He didn't have to wait long for her climax to hit, and when it did, he glanced up in time to see her tip her head back as she cried out, the pain of her nails scoring his shoulders nothing in comparison to the bliss of her climaxing beneath his mouth.

He licked her until she came down from her orgasm. Before she could collapse, he picked her up in his arms and plunked her onto the center of the mattress.

She flung her body back against the pillows with a groan. "You've got skills," she said as she struggled to catch her breath.

He laughed, liking this girl. "I'll take that as a compliment." He pushed his sweats down over his hips, freeing his rigid erection, then kicking the pants to the pile on the floor.

Gripping himself hard, he closed his eyes to gather himself, and when he opened them, she was staring with a hungry expression on her face.

"Jesus, Chloe. Stop looking at me like that or we're not going to make it to the good part."

"I already had my good part. I'm waiting for you to top yourself."

Her laughter rushed over him, and he groaned before opening the nightstand drawer and pulling out a condom. He didn't bring women to his private sanctuary, but he kept protection here to grab before he went out on a night when he needed or expected to find relief.

Ripping open the foil, he tossed the wrapper aside and rolled the condom over his straining dick before climbing onto the bed. She bent her knees, and he lifted one, pressing it back against her stomach as he knelt over her and settled his cock at her wet entrance.

He couldn't decide where he wanted to focus his gaze, on her beautiful face or the sight of her taking him deep inside of her. In the end, he couldn't tear his gaze from their joined bodies, and as he entered her, the fit was so perfect his eyes nearly rolled back in his head. And then he was buried completely, and he glanced into her blue eyes, hazy with desire.

He shifted his hips and settled even deeper. Her inner walls clasped around him, holding him tight, and her lashes fluttered closed. "So good."

"Fucking perfect," he muttered before gliding out, thrusting in again, picking up a punishing rhythm she had no problem arching up and meeting. Sex sounds surrounded them. Her moans, his grunts, desire rushing through him so fast he had a hard time keeping up.

He was more concerned that she kept pace, and he slowed only to have her grasp his face in her hands.

"Harder please," she said, and soon he was pounding into her.

From the cries echoing around him, he had no doubt she was going to come again, and he waited for her to shatter before he let loose the rest of the way. His balls drew up tight, and as she came, she took him along with her.

Jesus fuck. He'd never felt anything like that before in his life. Sprawling on top of her, he struggled to catch his breath, and beneath him, she did the same.

"So that's what makeup sex is like." Chloe opened her eyes and met his gaze. "Pretty impressive if I do say so myself."

Lost inside her, everything had been perfect, but now, with awareness came panic. God, he'd felt too much, and that hadn't been part of the plan.

It couldn't happen.

He wouldn't allow it and separated their bodies, rolling onto his back without replying.

Chloe stared at him in confusion, and he didn't know how to answer her. Instead he stood, removed the condom, and walked to the bathroom to toss it in the trash before heading back to find her putting on her clothes without looking his way.

Shit. "What are you doing?"

"Making sure you don't freak out. Or should I say freak out even more?" She snapped her jeans and pulled on her camisole, gathering the rest of her things.

He dropped his shoulders and realized he was being an ass. There was no reason this couldn't be exactly what they'd agreed on. Fun while it lasted. Even if that meant double pleasure in one night. Or her falling asleep in his bed and his arms.

"Come back," he said, sitting down on the mattress.

She shook her head. "I already told you, I know what this is and what it isn't. I also know what I want and need. You can relax, Beck. Linc isn't going to show up with a shotgun and demand you marry me. I'll see you in the morning."

She walked out and shut the door, with him cursing himself the entire time.

Chapter Six

CHLOE HADN'T SLEPT well thanks to what had felt like Beck's rejection, but this morning was different. She woke up with a whole new attitude. Beck pulling away hadn't hurt her feelings, or so she told herself. She was just coming off a broken engagement and being left at the altar. All she needed at the moment was mind-blowing sex. And sex with Beck had been just that. Not to mention exhilarating. It would only be life-altering if she allowed it. She wouldn't.

With last night behind her, today she was determined to return to the world. She showered, put on makeup, and chose one of her favorite new outfits, a pair of skinny black jeans, Chanel flats, and a white man-style shirt she tucked into the front. Leaving her hair down in natural waves, she pulled up half in JLo style and checked the mirror.

As it was the first time she'd be leaving the house since *it* had happened, if one camera caught her, she wanted everyone to know Owen hadn't destroyed her. She'd taken the time she needed to lick her wounds, and now she was a woman with a plan.

She might not want to go back to work with Linc, but she needed a place where she could concentrate and hoped Beck would let her come to his offices to work on her submission for the design contest. She also wanted to start apartment hunting. After last night, she couldn't stay here much longer without losing her head and her heart.

Walking to the kitchen, she heard the sound of Beck's voice, and it was obvious he was on a business call. She focused on her phone, looking at social media while she waited, giving him privacy.

Scrolling through Instagram, she came upon a picture of Owen walking into a trendy restaurant with a woman who was Chloe's exact opposite. Stick thin where Chloe had curves, brunette to her blonde, shoulder-length hair to her longer locks, and more petite for sure. His arm was around her – PDA that he'd never indulged in with Chloe – and in a way that signaled deep feelings, and the photographer had caught them looking into each other's eyes.

She swallowed hard. Why hadn't she thought to block him? Frozen, she stared at the photo and forced herself to think. It wasn't jealousy of the man himself—she'd accepted that theirs had been a comfort match—and it wasn't shock that he was with someone. He'd been up front about why he'd been a no-show at the wedding. But she hadn't gotten over the callous way he'd handled things, and she'd never seen such happiness on his face. Not when he'd been with her.

"Chloe?" Beck called her name from the entryway to the kitchen. "Are you okay? I was heading back to my room, and I called your name twice. You're just standing there in shock."

Swallowing hard, she turned her phone screen his way. "You know, it's not that I want him back. It's that…" She trailed off, unwilling to finish the sentence out loud.

Owen had something she feared she'd never find. Joy. Contentment. And the knowledge that the right person was in his orbit and reciprocated all those heady feelings of true love.

"It's that what?" Beck asked in a gentle voice.

She couldn't meet his gaze, nor would she finish her sentence. She'd told him she wanted a fun affair and she'd meant it, but she'd also denied being a woman who ultimately desired marriage.

She'd lied.

But after the incredible experience they'd shared, he'd withdrawn into himself and run away from, not toward, her. Beckett "I don't do relationships" Daniels was not the man for her.

"Nothing important." She snatched back her

phone. "Have you heard from your parents yet?"

His expression told her he knew she was avoiding discussing her ex with him. "No. If Mom reaches the doctor when the office opens, it should be soon. She said they start answering the phone at eight thirty."

She nodded. "I'm going to eat something, but I was hoping I could come to the office with you? Maybe you have an extra office or space where I can do some sketching?"

If he hadn't shut down on her last night, she'd have shared her contest entry and dreams for the future. She knew he'd be proud that she had taken his suggestion and conquered her fear. Now she just wanted to give him what she'd offered and no more. A roommate with occasional benefits.

He appeared to think and then nodded slowly. "Yes. We have a place where you can set up. A small conference room that can act as an office. Will that work for you?"

She nodded. "Yes, thanks." She needed to be away from the stifling offices where she hadn't been able to express herself, and she no longer wanted to hide away from the world.

"What are you working on?"

She opened her mouth to answer with some kind of avoidance and excuse when his cell rang.

Shooting her an apologetic glance, he pulled his

phone out of his pocket and glanced at the screen. He turned pale as he hit the accept button. "Mom?"

She didn't hesitate. Stepping closer, she put a hand on his shoulder, silently giving him support as he listened to the news.

★ ★ ★

BECK DISCONNECTED THE call with his mother and leaned back, needing the support of the wall behind him as much as he needed Chloe. Even as he didn't want to *need* anyone.

She stared at him, worry in her eyes. No matter how much of an ass he'd been to her, she wasn't walking away from him now. That showed her strength, and right now she had more than he did.

"Well?" she asked.

"Cancer." The word tasted sour in his mouth, and he still couldn't wrap his brain around the fact that they'd have to go through this horror again.

"Oh, Beck, I'm sorry." She stepped forward and pulled him into her arms, offering him comfort, and he wasn't tough enough not to take it. "What else do you know?" she asked.

"Mom didn't go into a lot of detail. Just that they caught it early. They think it's stage one, and they want him to see an oncologist, but they expect him to need more surgery around the area of the polyp that was removed. With luck, no treatment after. Yada, yada," he said, unable to help the sarcasm in his voice.

She narrowed her gaze. "Okay, we're going to sit down and talk." Grasping his hand, she pulled him down the hall and back to his room, pushing at him until he sat on the edge of the bed. "You said before you knew better than to trust what a doctor promises. Now this. Why are you so skeptical?"

He didn't answer immediately, not used to discussing his past.

"Okay, let's try this. How did your mother sound? Is she worried the doctors are wrong? Does she want a second opinion? Is she scared and disbelieving?" Chloe latched on to the subject and refused to let go.

He dipped his head. "Mom said she trusts the doctor and kept reassuring me Dad will be fine. But she was the same when Whitney was diagnosed." Shaking his head, he muttered a curse. "Shit."

Her hand rested on top of his. "Who's Whitney?" she asked, her tone gentle.

He groaned and forced himself to meet her gaze. "My sister. Tripp's twin. She died when she was sixteen. Leukemia."

Chloe gasped. "I had no idea. God, Beck. I'm sorry." Her hand curled tighter around his. "If you can't talk about it, I understand."

Silence descended between them, and once again,

he fought with himself over whether or not to reach out to her this way. Last night it had been about their physical connection. Telling her about Whitney now would create an emotional bond, the very thing he'd been trying to avoid.

"You know that my dad died suddenly," she said, taking over the conversation when he couldn't. "He had a heart attack. But what nobody knew was that he had the beginnings of dementia before that."

Beck winced. It wasn't the right time to get into the business mess that had recently occurred between him and Linc, and it wouldn't change anything with Chloe if he told her he'd heard rumors about her father's illness. Or about the land deal. It would just force a discussion of his history with her brother. And that was too much to add to today's heavy drama. So he let her continue.

"No matter how distant Dad was to my mom and us kids, I didn't want Dad – or any of us—to suffer watching him with that disease. And when he died, a part of me was grateful we wouldn't have to. And then I felt guilty for being glad he was gone." She was confiding in him, obviously encouraging him to do the same.

"I understand but you have nothing to feel guilty about." He glanced down at her hand still covering his and knew he was going to break and tell her about his sister.

He swallowed hard. "Whitney was Tripp's twin. He couldn't face watching her fade away, and Drew was busy with internships. I was there with her during treatments and after, when she'd get sick." He drew a deep breath before continuing. "The doctors said she had a good chance of beating it, and she believed them. My parents believed them. Everyone, including me, clung to that hope. Until it became obvious she wouldn't."

Chloe's hand came to his neck, her fingers threading up through his hair as she sat close and did the only thing she could. She listened.

"That's why I don't believe in doctors' platitudes. Words are easy. Statistics are just quotable numbers. Nobody really knows what's going to happen, and my experience with Whitney taught me to expect the worst."

Chloe sighed. "We both know there's nothing I can say that's going to change what happened to your sister. And I can't promise you that your father is going to be fine. But living without optimism isn't good for you. Expecting awful things and waiting for the worst to happen? All that means is that you'll miss out on the good things in between."

He heard her words. He just wasn't sure how to process them.

"Thank you for telling me," she said softly.

They sat in silence for a little while. The feel of her fingers against his scalp was mesmerizing and comforting, even as it was arousing. Something he wouldn't be acting on.

Not now.

Hell, he didn't know if being with her ever again was smart considering how deeply she got to him. This whole scene had been too intimate. "Let's go to the office," he said, rising to his feet.

She nodded. "Sounds like a plan. Let me get my things from my room. Oh, and can we stop somewhere for me to pick up breakfast? I never had a chance to eat, and I'm dying for some coffee."

She smiled and he was struck by how easily she allowed the subject change. She was so easy to be with, so understanding of his needs, be it distance or comfort. His princess was the perfect woman. For anyone other than him.

★ ★ ★

BY THE TIME they left to go to Beck's office, it was nine forty-five. On the way over by Uber, Chloe remained silent, giving him time to process what was going on with his father without adding her own problems to the things he needed to worry about. He'd given her a safe haven when she'd needed it, but he had his own life and issues, which meant it was time to move out of his apartment. She was ready. Now that she had a better understanding of what made Beck tick, she'd better be.

He was always braced for the worst, afraid of loss, and as a result, he put up walls. He didn't believe doctors' promises, and he didn't do relationships. It all made sense now, especially his pulling away last night. And though she didn't have to like it, she did need to respect his feelings.

They arrived at Beck's office, and she took in the fabulousness of the space. "I love the lobby," she said as they strode through the entry. The floors were polished concrete, the windows framed in black steel, and the fixtures a brushed brass.

"Thank you. I'm pretty damned proud of it," he said.

She shook her head and laughed. "As you should be."

They stepped into the elevator and headed up to the top floor, where a woman sat behind a marble desk. "Good morning, Mr. Daniels."

He smiled. "Morning, Annabelle. This is my friend Chloe Kingston. If she needs anything, please make sure she gets it."

"My pleasure. Nice to meet you, Chloe," the pretty brunette said.

"Same," Chloe said with a warm smile.

From there, the tour encompassed the break room, Beck telling her there was a cafeteria downstairs, and introducing her to his personal assistant, who she asked about wirelessly hooking up a printer to her laptop.

The attractive redhead named Ronnie promised to come by the conference room and make sure she had the password for the internet. She also said she'd help her get her computer set up to print.

Beck showed her to her workspace, a small room where she settled in. She'd been perfecting her contest entry for months prior to taking the leap and entering. The written component included a fifty-word project summary and a challenge statement, which was essentially a guiding statement to make the client trust in her work. To prove she had a deeper understanding of their needs while incorporating the balance, flow, and rhythm, along with the proportion and scale of the project.

Every time she revisited her entry, she found herself making changes to the challenge and the solutions. There was also such a thing as taking the point of view and uniqueness out of something, and if she kept tweaking, she risked her entry becoming too generic. Too much like the designs for Linc she wanted to leave behind.

Ronnie had come in and hooked her up to the internet and printer as promised, and Chloe had been working for over an hour. Needing a break, she turned her attention to apartment hunting. Linc would help her in a heartbeat if she asked him, but she wanted to find a place to live on her own.

Picking up her cell, she called a friend who was a Realtor and explained the type of place she wanted. Amelia promised to send listings to look at later today.

Chloe had to admit she hated the idea of moving out of Beck's loft. Not only did she love the space and décor, she enjoyed his company. He'd been a good friend and source of support, but he'd revealed why she couldn't rely on him long-term, and hearing his reasons why? She knew she'd better believe him.

A couple of hours passed during which Chloe, despite her internal warning, perfected her writing portion even more. Her Realtor friend sent rental openings along with some condominiums for her to check out. She printed the ones that looked the most promising because she wanted to see the layouts in larger format.

Then she headed to the break room, took one look at the Keurig, and decided she'd much rather have a Starbucks instead. She'd seen one across the street, and she just needed to get her phone that had her app so she could pay.

She walked into the conference room to find Beck staring at her screen, the 3D model of the studio she was designing open for him to see.

"Beck?"

He turned to face her. If she thought the man had been sexy prior to her sleeping with him, she found him even more so now. Ignoring the tug of attraction wasn't easy, but she'd made herself a promise to pull back.

"This is a phenomenal transformation," he said, his gaze never returning to the screen. "You turned a bland, open room into a multifunctional living space." He leaned in closer. "Love the glass panel partition," he mused. "It lets natural light illuminate the whole apartment."

She warmed at his enthusiasm. She couldn't remember the last time Linc had been excited by her designs or work. Not because he didn't like the job she did. He never hesitated to compliment her, but this kind of exhilaration was different.

"Yes." She stepped up beside Beck. "The average studio apartment is five hundred and fourteen square feet, so I needed to make use of every last inch without leaving it cluttered. Look." She pointed her finger without touching the screen. "I hid a foldaway Murphy bed that has shelf storage when closed, and I used mirrors to give the illusion of more room," she said.

"Is that wall a deep purple?" he asked.

"A dark violet accent wall."

"Hmm."

She was unable to get a read on whether or not he liked the color she'd chosen. Suddenly, something she'd kept secret for so long was in the open, and it felt like she was exposing her heart and soul.

"I like it," he said at last.

And with his approval, she realized how much she'd wanted him to admire her designs. His validation mattered because she'd had so little in her life. Oh, her brothers wanted what was best for her, in that big-brother-knows-what-that-is sort of way. But Beck was separate and apart from her family. Not only did his opinion matter, *he* mattered.

So much for emotional distance, she thought, frustrated with herself.

"Who is this for? Because it can't be Linc. Not with the ultramodern accents." He turned to face her, curiosity in his gaze.

She drew a deep breath. "Do you remember when we talked about reaching for what we want? And I asked about fear?"

A knowing smile lifted his sensual lips. "Yes. And I said to go out, grab the world by the balls, and go after it, anyway."

She nodded. "I did. Have you heard of Elevate's

Online Interior Design Professionals Contest?"

He nodded. "Our in-house interior designer has mentioned it along with the perks that come with winning. I didn't want to lose her, so I paid her more to stay and not compete." He shrugged. "In case she won and ended up with a job that would take her away from us. Couldn't let that happen."

Chloe laughed, admiring his cocky attitude and business sense. "Well, I already sent in my entry form. And this is my planned submission," she said, waving a hand toward the laptop, heart pounding in her chest at the admission.

For some people, submitting wasn't a big deal. For Chloe it meant taking that huge step toward independence.

"You did? That's fantastic!" He turned toward her, lifted her off her feet, and spun her around in celebration. "Congratulations!"

As he lowered her, their bodies rubbed together, and awareness shot through her, causing her nipples to harden beneath her shirt. Thank God it was oversized, she thought, glad he couldn't see the effect he had on her.

"When are you going to send it in?" he asked, voice gruff, indicating he'd felt the same sparks she had.

Forcing herself to focus on his question wasn't

easy when her body was on fire. "I'll enter when I stop trying to make it perfect," she admitted.

He narrowed his gaze. "How close to final is it?"

Even she couldn't deny the truth. "It's there. Every new tweak will take the individuality out of it." She rubbed her hands up and down her arms, her nerves showing again.

He braced his hands on her shoulders. "Then what do you say you submit now? And tonight we go out to dinner to celebrate?"

"Really? Are you sure you're in the mood?" He'd had a blow this morning, and he'd been upset about his dad.

He inclined his head. "I can't change the diagnosis, right? Dwelling won't help. I'm going to see my parents this weekend. So yes, I'm sure. You need to go for what will make you happy, and we need to celebrate your accomplishment. Now no more stalling. Life's short."

His sister, she thought, understanding him so much better now. She could learn a lesson from his loss, too.

She clasped her hands in front of her. "The photos are set and formatted, captions and floor plans complete. The written section is also finished." She nibbled on her lower lip. "You're right. It's time."

Grinning, he took her hand and pulled her closer

to the laptop. "Good. You're ready to show them what you've got."

It helped to have him in her corner, cheering her on. He was in the real estate business, was aware of design and aesthetic, and she trusted he wouldn't let her make a fool of herself.

Her heart slammed inside her chest as she pulled out the chair and sat down in front of the screen. Beck's firm hand never left her back as she closed out of the program she'd been working in and began the submission process.

★ ★ ★

BECK FELT THE tension in the room. From Chloe's stiff shoulders to the way her hands trembled as she hit the keys, he knew this move was taking everything she had inside her. And he was so damned proud of her.

Had he pushed? Yes, but nowhere she didn't want to go. She'd just needed the right encouragement.

With the last tap of a key, they watched, waiting for the confirmation to appear on the screen. When it happened, she screenshotted the words. "And done!" She spun around to face him, eyes wide, cheeks flushed. "I did it!"

"Yes!" He fist-pumped the air. "Go, Chloe!" he said, pulling her to her feet. "How do you feel?"

She treated him to a wide smile, the truest he'd seen since meeting her at her non-wedding.

"I feel free! I've been so worried about feeling like a failure if I don't win or even final, but now that it's done? So what if I don't? I'll find something else and try again. I have dreams and I'm entitled to them." Her eyes shone with certainty.

"That's my girl," he said. "I mean…"

She shook her head. "It's fine. I know what you mean." She stepped away, obviously putting distance between them.

Distance he'd put there first. He needed to get his shit together when it came to Chloe and fast. Push-pull wasn't his style.

He cleared his throat. "Just so you know, design professionals judge the contest, and there's a good chance someone will notice your work regardless of where you place."

Her eyes shone bright. "I can't tell you how much I appreciate your belief in me. It's been a while since anyone trusted in my skills. Not that my brothers aren't great guys but–"

"They have their own ideas of what's best for you. I get it. I think if Whitney had lived, the three of us would be the same way." He let out a deep breath, surprised at how much better he felt admitting that out loud.

He never talked about Whitney. He kept everything bottled up inside him, safe and sound, memories he could take out and hold when he wanted to and push away when they hurt too much. He'd always believed looking at them in the light of day would be too painful to bear, but that admission hadn't hurt quite the way he would have thought.

"Hey, are you okay?" Chloe grasped his hands, her cool palms bringing him back to the present.

He blinked and focused on her beautiful face. "Yeah. I'm good."

"Okay then." She smiled. "Were you serious about going out for dinner?"

"Yes." He'd have Ronnie make them a reservation. "Definitely."

"Then would you mind if I went back to the loft to pull myself together? I can meet you at the restaurant if it's easier."

His gaze slid over her outfit, skinny black jeans with a white men's shirt that shouldn't look hot on her but did. And with her wavy hair pulled away from her face, he remembered what she'd looked like last night, his cock hard inside her, her soft body beneath his.

He cleared his throat. "I'll come pick you up. Don't worry about it. I had plans to have a quick drink with my brothers around six. Is eight o'clock too late?"

She shook her head. "Not at all." She closed her

laptop and gathered her things. "I'll call an Uber."

"Let me call you a car," he said at the same time.

She laughed, her mood still obviously light. "I can get my own ride but thanks. See you tonight."

She bounced out of the room and he watched her go, hair swinging behind her. His dick was hard in his pants, and his brain was on overdrive, confusion about what to do with his mixed feelings for her swirling in his head. Hence the drinks with his brothers. They knew nothing about meeting him, but he'd call them now. Because he needed them to help him sort his shit.

He glanced at the table and caught sight of papers Chloe had left there. He stepped forward to grab them to give them to her later when he saw the top page.

Realty listings.

Chloe was looking to move out.

★ ★ ★

FOR THE REST of the day, Beck felt the gut punch of Chloe wanting to leave, which made no sense to him when he was actively keeping her at a distance. Luckily his brothers were more than willing to meet up after work, and at six p.m., he walked into Club TEN29, an upscale nightclub not far from his loft that was also open for drinks after work.

Beck had met the three owners when he'd rented

them the building on property he owned. The men had made a huge success of their business since they'd opened four years ago, and Beck respected them for it. He spent time here with friends or his siblings when he wanted to relax early in the evening or make a night of it later on.

Since he wanted to talk to Tripp and Drew, he chose a table instead of a seat at the bar and waited for them to join him. He looked at the glass taking up the entire back wall that was lined with liquor bottles, admiring the view.

"Hey." Jason Dare, one of the club owners, strode over. He owned the club with two of his fraternity brothers, Tanner Grayson and Landon Bennett, and had named it in honor of Landon's brother, who died years ago during a frat hazing gone wrong.

"Hey, Beck. It's been awhile. How've you been?" Jason asked, walking up to him.

"Busy as usual. You?"

Jason shrugged. "The same. Except…" He paused, a grin on his face, making Beck curious.

"Except what?"

"My wife is pregnant," Jason said, obviously just waiting for the opening to share the news.

Beck rose from his seat and slapped the other man on the back. "That's great! Congratulations!"

Jason nodded. "So can I buy you"—he glanced

over Beck's shoulder—"and your brothers a drink to celebrate? I'm feeling generous these days."

Beck chuckled because he and the guys always argued over Beck's need to pay, which was ridiculous. He was their landlord and friend, but he ought to pay as much as anyone else who frequented the bar.

Tripp and Drew had joined them at the tail end of the conversation.

"His wife is pregnant," Beck explained to his siblings.

"Congratulations," Tripp and Drew said at the same time.

"Thank you. Now, what can I get for you? Your usual Macallan?" Jason asked.

"That'd be great. And give that beautiful wife of yours my best," Beck said.

"Same from us." Tripp spoke for himself and Drew.

The guys settled into chairs and Beck sat back down. He and his brothers played catch-up about each other's work for a few minutes, until a cocktail waitress brought over a bottle of scotch and glasses.

"Mr. Dare said to enjoy. He had to handle something but said he'll see you later." She served them and walked away, leaving them alone again.

"Now that we have fortification…" Tripp said, "what's going on? I'm guessing this impromptu meet has something to do with your houseguest?" He lifted his glass. "To Dad's health."

"Amen," Beck said, touching his glass to theirs while they did the same.

Beck took a long drink as he considered how to reply.

"I bet Chloe's rocked his world, and he doesn't know what to do with her. Is that it?" Drew asked, meeting Beck's gaze.

And Beck already regretted calling these two to talk. It wasn't like either sibling was currently in a relationship or anything. He should have just figured out his problem by himself.

"Okay, sorry, man. You obviously have something on your mind." Drew folded his arms and leaned on the table. "Talk."

Beck frowned but his options were limited. His brothers were all he had. "Fine. Yeah, I slept with her, and now I feel like I'm playing that push-pull game. Which I don't mean to do. It's not fair to her. It's just that she's different than anyone I've been with before." Needing a drink, he took another sip, savoring the burn as it went down.

"Is she pushing you for more than you're willing to give?" Tripp, who was just coming off of a breakup, asked.

Beck shook his head. "Not at all. I told her from

the start I don't do relationships, and she said she wasn't looking to jump into another one."

"Then what's the problem?" Drew asked. "Sounds to me like you're the one making things more complicated than they need to be."

And wasn't that a kick in the ass? Beck downed a larger sip of his drink.

"What's going on?" Tripp pushed.

"She makes me feel things," he muttered, not in the least bit happy with himself.

A smirk edged Tripp's mouth. "Well, I'll be damned."

"What are you going to do about it?" Drew asked.

Beck rolled his head to ease the tension in his shoulders. "Look, nothing's changed. I don't want to get seriously involved with anyone. You both know why and I'm not getting into it again now. But the fact that Dad's sick? Just reinforces how right I am in my thinking." He downed the last of his drink.

Drew lifted the bottle and poured him another glass.

Beck shook his head. "I don't need another. I have dinner plans." With Chloe."

"Listen." Tripp leaned forward and spoke in that calming doctor voice that could get annoying. "Chloe's not staying with you forever, so just have fun while she's there. Spell out those terms so she understands

That'll avoid you overthinking, not to mention the hot-cold thing you don't want to keep doing." He shrugged. "Simple."

More than Tripp knew, since Chloe already planned on moving out.

"The man's got a point." Drew placed his glass down on the table. "Not that I necessarily agree with your thinking about forever. Look at Mom and Dad, the things they've survived together. Makes me think someone for the long haul might not be so bad."

Beck's muscles stiffened at the notion. "I don't agree with you. It's just one more person to love … and possibly lose." He cleared his throat. "But Tripp's idea makes sense." And it helped ease the knot building in his chest.

Changing his mind, he picked up his glass and took a final sip, still weighing his options, ultimately deciding Tripp was right. If he put a limit on this thing with Chloe, he could handle it without hurting either one of them. And that's what he'd keep telling himself until he believed it.

Chapter Seven

Beck planned to take Chloe to the exclusive club he belonged to in the heart of the Hudson Yards. Only the elite could be members, and Beck didn't say that lightly. It was the crown jewel of private social clubs. Booking a private room here, where no one else would see them or have access, was something he'd never considered before and probably never would again. Michelin star chefs and staff that were vetted and arguably the best in the world were at his disposal.

He'd made the decision before Tripp had imparted his wise words about how to handle things with Chloe because Beck wanted to treat her to the best. Yes, her family could afford access, and for all he knew, Linc was a member. Beck didn't keep track of the who's who on the roster. But his gut told him nobody had treated Chloe like the princess she'd dressed as the night of her aborted wedding. He intended to do just that and refused to question why.

Before heading to meet with his brothers, he'd texted her and told her to wear the nicest dress she had in the closet. He'd followed it up with, if she didn't have a fancy dress at his place, have one sent over. She was going to need it, and he knew Chloe had the connections to be ready when he returned.

By the time he walked into his loft, it was close to seven thirty, and he still wanted to take a shower and change. Today had felt much longer than planned.

He was tired, almost wishing he had no plans for the night. Until he saw Chloe. She stepped from the hall into the entryway, and one look blew him away. She wore a white, sleeveless, fitted dress that ended above the knee, hugging her slim waist and fuller hips. But it was the black leather straps that caught his attention. Leather ran around both the neckline and her shoulders, crisscrossing at the waist and stretching beneath her breasts. Breasts he'd held in his hands and tasted with his mouth.

His cock, already hard from looking at her, now stood at attention at the memory. He forced his gaze upward to her amused face, which was gorgeous. Her makeup accentuated her blue eyes, and her plush lips were a gorgeous pink. He slipped a hand into his front pocket and not so subtly adjusted himself.

She graced him with a knowing smile. "Are you going to say something or just stare at me all night? Because really, either way works for me."

He grinned, stepping forward and taking her hand.

"You look gorgeous, Chloe. Take-my-breath-away gorgeous."

Those lips lifted in a pleased smile. "Glad you like."

He so fucking did. "I need to take a quick shower and I'll be ready to go."

She nodded. "Hurry up. I'm hungry."

Another thing he liked about Chloe Kingston. She didn't hide the fact that she appreciated food. "Don't worry. I have a special night planned that will satisfy all your desires." With a wink, he headed off to shower. And probably to take the edge off before he sat through a long dinner before they got to dessert.

★ ★ ★

CHLOE GLANCED AT the man she had no business ogling no matter how hot he looked in his black slacks, matching jacket, and a white shirt, unbuttoned at the neck. Freshly showered, he smelled delicious, with a hint of his musky after shave surrounding her in the Rolls Royce Phantom Limousine on the way to dinner.

Not just a limousine but an icon her brothers used. Of course, Dash, the rock star, would want to make an entrance, and Xander, the thriller writer, desired space and privacy. Linc just enjoyed the good things. Beck had splurged, and knowing how much he liked to use a ride share and not act like the rich man he was, she more than appreciated the gesture.

The venue? A club her father and her brother also belonged to, but she'd never been here. Linc wasn't much of a socializer, but he had the membership for wining and dining clients. All Chloe knew was that this was the most exclusive place in the city, and Beck had secured a private dining room just for them.

Which told her he was back to sending mixed signals.

"Beck," she said, picking up her champagne flute and taking a sip of the bubbly liquid. "I realize we don't know each other well, but there is something you should know about me."

"And what is that?" he asked, studying her. In fact, he could barely take his gaze off her, which meant her dress had accomplished its goal.

She'd wanted him to take notice. Needed him to understand she wasn't the crying woman he'd rescued or the needy female who'd hidden out in his loft for a week. She was not only finding herself but standing up for what she wanted as well.

"I don't play games and I'm hoping you don't either."

"Looks like you're going to beat me to this conversation." Although he'd taken a sip of champagne after toasting to her bravery and hopeful success, he'd also ordered Macallan on the rocks and took a drink of that now.

Not willing to make whatever he wanted to discuss too easy on him, she waited in silence. After all, he'd been the one to turn to ice last night only to be totally different again this morning. If he'd given it thought, she wanted to hear what he had to say.

He leaned back in his seat, holding his drink. "I told you about my sister."

She nodded, the urge to take his hand and comfort him strong, but she waited.

"Whitney had this … let's call it a bucket list of things she wanted to do when she recovered … and turned eighteen, because let's face it. For ideas like sky jumping, hot air ballooning, and seeing the northern lights, she needed my parents' permission. Or to be an adult." A muscle ticked in his jaw but he continued. "When it became obvious she wasn't going to get better, she made me promise I'd do all the things on her list."

He placed his glass on the table, and unable to help herself, she reached over and put her hand over his. He shot her a grateful look.

She couldn't believe how insightful his sister had been, so young. But then looking at a potentially terminal illness would make anyone grow up fast. Chloe was so sad, both for the girl who'd never had the chance to live out her dreams and for Beck, who was obviously so destroyed by losing her.

"Anyway," he said, picking up the thread of conversation. "I promised I'd do all those things myself if we couldn't do them together, and I did. Mostly. Except for the northern lights and the last thing on her list."

"Which is?" Chloe asked, curious and with a lump in her throat thanks to his story.

He met her gaze. "Fall in love and get married." He slid his hand from beneath hers.

She opened and closed her mouth again but had no idea what to say.

"Thing is, I'd already promised myself I wouldn't add anyone to the list of people I care about so deeply that losing them would break me." His entire body looked taut, his muscles tense, and he appeared suddenly ready to bolt.

But she'd gotten the message and both understood and accepted the reason behind it. "So no relationships," she said. "And no messy falling in love or getting married." Why did her stomach hurt with those words?

He inclined his head. "Last night was … intense and I had a freak-out moment. But I've given it a lot of thought and it's all on me. You said you weren't looking for anything serious, either, so I had no reason to go cold on you."

She took a longer sip of champagne, considering her options, gathering her thoughts. "I meant it. I'm not interested in a relationship either." And she really shouldn't be given she was just getting back on her feet.

He studied her face, as if assessing whether or not she was telling him the truth. Obviously he believed her because he visibly relaxed.

"Which means there's no reason we can't continue to have fun while you're staying with me. If that's what you want." He lifted one eyebrow and waited, his words hanging between them.

By suggesting they continue to sleep together and by putting a time limit on things, he'd taken her off guard. Again.

Did she want to hook up with Beck until she moved out? Yes, she did. Even if she had to be very careful with her emotions because she already felt something for this man who'd obviously lost a piece of himself when his sister died and was too afraid to rebuild by letting other people in.

"Is that what this is all about?" She waved a hand around the room. "The exclusive club, the private room, piped-in music, fancy clothes … are you wining and dining me in the hopes of convincing me to sleep with you again, Mr. Daniels?" Because she had to admit, if so, he was trying pretty hard.

A sexy grin lifted his lips. "Actually, no. I'm doing this because you deserve it. You took a big step, and you ought to have it acknowledged and celebrated." He slid his fingers through hers and kissed the back of her hand. "And no matter what you decide about us, we are going to do just that."

She blinked. He continually managed to surprise her and she sighed. How was she supposed to keep her feelings casual when he did sweet things, like caring about what she needed and believed she deserved?

There was no way she could turn down his suggestion. She'd take whatever time she could have with him and enjoy it while she could. "You have yourself a deal," she murmured. "Until I move out."

His gorgeous green eyes stared into hers. "Which you plan to do soon? Because you left a list of rental units in the conference room, and I want you to know there's no rush to leave."

She couldn't help but smile even as she shook her head. There were those mixed signals again. "I think it's best if I start looking. It's time I stand on my own two feet." She paused. "But in the meantime, I think we should make the most of the time we have left."

"And I agree." He touched his glass to hers then pushed his chair back and stood. "What are you doing?"

"Getting comfortable." He walked over to the booth where she sat across from him and slid in beside her. He extended his arm behind her, and his roughened fingers grazed her bare shoulder.

Her entire body flooded with heat, and arousal spiked inside her. She wasn't sure what she'd expected, but with the heavy discussion out of the way, she was able to relax and enjoy. Even with him sitting close and her being so physically aware of him, their back-and-forth banter was easy and light.

She and Beck had shared time together since she'd moved in, and she'd learned a lot about him. He preferred suspense thrillers to comedies in both movies and books, holding a print copy in his hand over an e-reader, would pick reading over TV, and had no patience for binge watching. She, on the other hand, would choose a romantic comedy any time, liked to read romance on a tablet or her phone, and she also didn't enjoy bingeing television shows and losing hours at a time.

But tonight wasn't about the mundane. Tonight was the first night they were exclusively focused on each other in a way that allowed the sexual tension to be present and bubble over. And despite their friendship, which she knew was real, she heard innuendo in everything they said or did, from the moment he'd pushed back his chair and slid into her curved booth.

Including the fact that oysters were the first course.

He held one out for her to suck from the shell, and she did, her gaze never leaving his heavy-lidded one as she chewed and swallowed. She was then forced to watch his throat move as he did the same, and a yearning hit her hard, her panties growing damp just watching him.

Unfortunately she had three more courses to go, but she enjoyed every one. A salad consisting of arugula with pears and prosciutto, duck breast with sweet cherry sauce for the main course, and the most decadent chocolate souffle with vanilla bean ice cream. All accompanied by Bling H2O, poured from a limited-edition frosted-glass bottle, covered with hand-applied Swarovski crystals.

As privileged as her life had been, a fifty-dollar bottle of water was over-the-top, even for her. But she appreciated the sentiment of this meal and would never forget that he'd done this to make her feel special.

Their conversation drifted from how his parents were handling his father's diagnosis – Beck wouldn't know for sure until he went there for dinner tomorrow night – to whether she had business ideas in mind in case she didn't win the competition. She found herself telling him about wanting to open a design shop where she could choose her own clients who had vision similar to those Chloe enjoyed creating. Once again he supported her and offered any help she needed. No questions asked.

At which point she was relaxed and comfortable enough that the words just came out of her mouth. "So what happened between you and Linc? One time I visited and you two were living together and best friends, then I heard you moved out and he never mentioned it again. Until you both ended up as real estate competitors."

Beck froze, obviously shocked by the question. "We had a falling-out," he finally said.

Well, if that wasn't vague, she thought with frustration. "I assumed you had. I take it you won't tell me over what?" She'd been taking tiny bites of her souffle and put the fork down, deciding she couldn't eat another morsel.

"It wasn't over *what*. It was over *who*." He rubbed his hands together before finally meeting her gaze. "And as much as I would like to explain, out of respect for you and your relationship with your brother, it's not my story to tell."

"You argued over a girl?" she asked, putting the pieces together. She was surprised because that thought hadn't crossed her mind.

"Chloe … don't push me on this. You need to talk to Linc."

Beck set his jaw in what she'd come to think of as the expression he used when he wouldn't budge.

"Trust me, okay? If I thought I should explain things, I would," he said.

"But you won't because you're protecting my relationship with Linc." She didn't understand how but she'd accept his request. "Okay."

"Thank you. So did you have that dress, or did you ask one of your personal shoppers to send it over?" he asked, his irises darkening as his gaze came to rest on her breasts, pushed up slightly by the ribbing beneath them.

Accepting the change of subject, she grinned. "What do you think?"

He ran his finger along the leather strip, and her entire body trembled at his touch, which deliberately included the undersides of her breasts. "I think you wanted something special just for me." His thumbs brushed over her distended nipples, hard and aroused from his teasing touch. "And I appreciate the effort because I can't stop staring." His gaze was hot and still focused on her chest.

Despite being completely covered, exposing no cleavage, this dress managed to tease, and that was exactly what she'd wanted.

"Would you like more dessert?" he asked.

"No, thank you." She shook her head and sighed.

"This was the best meal I've ever had."

Beck's answering smile warmed her inside.

"That was the plan," he said. "And since we're both full, let's dance before we head home."

Full or not, she was all too willing to rub her body against his sexy one.

He slid out of the booth and extended his hand, helping her stand in her high heels. As if he'd choreographed it, the music became a notch louder, and he pulled her into his arms.

For the first few minutes, he held her in a respectful position as they swayed in time to the music, but the longer the song went on, the more intimate they became. His hand moved to her lower back, and then his fingers dipped to cover her ass and pull her against his hard body, the swell of his erection obvious and thick against her sex.

"I haven't danced in a while," he murmured in her ear.

Her hands came to his shoulders. "This no longer feels like just dancing," she said, and his low chuckle reverberated inside her.

"That's because it isn't. It's foreplay."

The word sent a zing straight to her clit. "Not nice when you know we have a twenty-minute ride home." And she was already soaking wet for him.

"The limo has a soundproof partition." Dipping

his head, he settled his lips against her neck, nuzzling behind her ear before nipping at her lobe.

Her nipples tightened even more, and she rubbed herself against his erection, causing a powerful quiver to pulse through her, and she dug fingernails into the material of his jacket.

"We need to go." Her knees were already weak at the thought of having him inside her soon.

His green eyes, blazing with heat, met hers, and he treated her to a curt nod. "We do."

Grasping her hand, he started for the door, pausing only long enough to let her grab her purse before they were rushing for the limo outside.

★ ★ ★

BECK DIDN'T KNOW what it was about Chloe, but she pulled him in, bringing them closer without him meaning to let it happen. She was just so damned easy to talk to. Comforting about his dad, curious about his life and work, and down-to-earth despite her upbringing. She didn't expect the best, was surprised when he provided it, and was utterly grateful for small favors.

Unlike many of the woman he'd dated, who had obviously been with him for the money and perks that came with it. Which was why he rarely went out with anyone more than twice. Three times, max. He'd heard his brothers use the word *fuck buddy*, and though he understood the meaning, he'd always been too concerned a woman would assume anything beyond a second date meant real interest on his part.

Though there were probably females he could trust, there were more women who claimed to be fine with a casual, sex-only situation, but deep down they hoped to be the one to change him.

Yet here he was, in over his head with Chloe Kingston. The irony was, when she said she wasn't ready for a relationship so soon after her broken engagement, he believed her. But he also knew whatever this thing was between them, it went deeper than *just sex*. And wouldn't that make her brother happy, he thought, aware of the irony.

She'd asked about his broken relationship with Linc, but he didn't regret not answering. If all he wanted to do was stick it to Linc, he'd have spilled the whole sordid story and dimmed her view of her oldest sibling. But he cared more about her feelings than taking down Linc in any sort of revenge scheme. That wasn't in his nature. Torturing him a little? Sure. But that wasn't why he wanted Chloe with him for now.

He cut off his thoughts as they approached the limousine and the driver hopped out to open the door and let them inside. Chloe slid in first.

"Please drive around until I let you know we're ready to go home," Beck instructed the man who was paid as much to be discreet as he was to chauffeur.

"Yes, sir."

Beck climbed in and the door shut behind him. He immediately hit the button, closing the partition and choosing the opaque sheeting. Enclosed in luxury and silence, he turned to Chloe. She had a bad-girl gleam in her eye, and before he could consider his next move, she'd hiked up her dress and straddled him, her knees on either side of his thighs.

He slipped his hand between them, and his breath caught at the wetness he found there. "Jesus."

She brushed her lips over his at the same time her hips rocked forward, her pussy grinding over the bulge in his pants, and his cock grew even harder. He hoped he could hold out and curled one hand into a fist. The minx repeated the motion, and a wave of desire flooded his system.

He closed his eyes and groaned. "I'm not going to survive until I'm inside you."

She jerked at the sentiment. Was it his imagination or did his words make her even wetter?

"I have a solution to take the edge off," she said in a husky voice.

"Yeah?" He pushed her hair off her shoulders and gathered the long strands in one hand. "And what would that be?"

She slid backwards, forcing him to release her hair

as she dropped to her knees on the limo floor. Reaching up, she unhooked the button on his pants and eased the zipper over his aching cock. Her intent was more than he'd expected. Tonight was supposed to be about her.

Still, he lifted his ass, and she slid his pants and boxer briefs over his hips and pulled them down, settling herself between his parted legs. Then she lifted herself on her knees, wrapped her fingers around him, and slid her hand up and down his straining shaft.

He groaned at how good her warm grip felt and wasn't surprised when a drop of pre come pooled at the head. He closed his eyes to pull himself together, but when he felt the warm lap of her tongue, an animalistic sound escaped his throat.

Opening his eyes and looking down, he found her mouth wrapped around him, her eyes raised as she met his gaze. Needing to touch her and find some sort of control over a situation where, in reality, he had none, he wrapped his hand around her hair once more. As she began to suck him deep, he pulled on the long strands.

She moaned around his dick and it reverberated inside him.

"Touch yourself," he ordered her, knowing he wasn't going to last, not with those luscious lips enclosing him in wet heat.

He was vaguely aware of her free hand, which had been on his thigh, lowering to where he couldn't see. But he heard the rustle of material and her sudden trembling sigh. He envisioned her fingers, coated in her juices, sliding over her clit and moving in small circles that aroused her.

His imagination melded with reality, and her body began to jerk, her mouth on his cock becoming less steady.

Knowing she was sliding her fingers over the lips of her sex, his own desire grew hotter, higher, and faster. His entire being drew taut. Suddenly she stilled and shook as she cried out, coming hard, his cock aching as he waited out her climax.

His hand moved from tugging her hair to sliding gently over the soft strands. And then she was back, slipping a hand around the base of his cock and pumping up and down in time to the suction of her mouth. He pulled on her hair as she moved, pumping his hips until his balls drew up and he was going to come.

"Princess, move," he said, warning her, but she merely tightened her hold. Both her mouth and her hand gripped him harder, and she sucked him to the back of her throat.

Next thing he knew, all restraint was gone as his orgasm exploded, taking him over, pleasure filling him, as his long climax continued.

Not letting go, Chloe stayed with him, swallowing all he had to give and only releasing him when he collapsed against the back of the seat.

"Holy fuck," he muttered, completely spent.

Rising, she returned to the seat beside him.

He rolled his head to the side, meeting her hazy gaze. Her lips were red and puffy, a look of sated satisfaction on her face. She shifted her dress and pulled the hem back down, her breaths still coming hard and fast.

"Are you okay?" he asked.

She leaned back against the seat. "Never better, and I mean that." Her expression softened. "There's something to be said for mutual satisfaction."

He narrowed his gaze, well aware there were many ways for him to take that comment, none of them good for her. Even though her pleasure had come at her own hand, he'd demanded it, and they'd come nearly at the same time. He had a strong hunch that had rarely happened for her before now.

Acting on instinct, he slid a hand around the back of her neck and pulled her in for a long, deep kiss. One he needed and hoped she did, too.

Once again shaken by the depth of emotion sex with Chloe brought, it took everything inside him not to pull back and be an asshole again. Instead he gave in to what he really wanted.

He picked up the phone and called the driver, instructing him to take them home. His bed was waiting and he wasn't finished with Chloe. Not by a long shot.

Chapter Eight

BACK AT THE apartment, Chloe kicked off her heels and was about to turn into her room when Beck grasped her wrist and tugged her into his bedroom.

"We're not finished," he said in a gruff voice.

Considering her body still tingled but felt surprisingly empty, she wasn't about to arguc. She dropped the shoes beside his big bed and sat down on the mattress. He'd already begun to undress. His shoes and socks were in a pile. He'd shrugged off his jacket, laying it on the dresser, and was in the process of unbuttoning his shirt.

Propping herself back on one hand, she decided to watch the show. As he shrugged off white material, his tanned skin came into view along with rippled muscles he must work hard to maintain.

"What do you do at the gym?" she asked, doing her best not to drool at the sight.

He grinned and started to take off his pants. "Treadmill for cardio, weights with a trainer, and a punching bag." Hooking his thumbs into the sides, he pulled off the slacks and boxer briefs, letting them fall and kicking them aside.

And if she thought she'd had an eyeful before, she had an even bigger one now. Much bigger, she thought, holding back an unladylike giggle. His sculpted chest tapered down to one of those sexy vees women loved so much and an arousal that let her know she wasn't alone with this heady desire rushing through her.

"Your turn," he said.

She shifted until she was on her knees and turned her back to him, pulling her hair out of the way. "Unzip me?"

He stepped up behind her, his body heat warm at her back as he unzipped the dress and pressed kisses against her neck and trailed down her spine. She shivered and her nipples pebbled into tight peaks, her arousal growing hotter and wetter.

With a flick of his wrist, he unhooked her bra. From there it was simple to shimmy off the dress and silk undergarment and let them pool at her knees. Wrapping his arms around her, he swiped his thumbs over her breasts. They were already sensitive, and she sucked in a shallow breath at his touch.

Next thing she knew, he'd picked her up, turned her around, and set her down on the bed, sliding her ass to the edge of the mattress. With the bed up on a platform, he had the perfect height to return the favor from the limo, and she wouldn't argue that he wanted to. She'd already experienced his talented mouth and tongue and wanted more.

Dropping to his knees, he spread her thighs and lowered his head until his tongue swiped at her sex. He lifted her legs over his shoulders and proceeded to devour her like a starving man. It didn't take long for him to send her flying, her climax fast and furious.

In the time it took for her to come back to herself, he had a condom on and was entering her, and her body responded all over again. This was harder and faster than their first time, the frenzy a result of the buildup all evening. Taking the edge off with an orgasm for each of them hadn't curbed their desire.

He thrust in and out, his pace unrelenting, and when he lifted her hips, the angle had him hitting her G-spot, the wash of sensation incredible, and she needed more.

"Again, Beck. Harder this time." Her fingers scrambled to grab the comforter, but before she could get a grip, Beck pulled out and pushed back in, over and over, until he was driving into her just as she'd asked.

She moaned and arched up, meeting him thrust for thrust, clasping her inner walls around his powerful erection.

"Fuck, Chloe, you feel good." His grip on her thighs tightened, and it wasn't long before she was soaring, her climax overwhelming her in the best possible way.

Three more thrusts and Beck's groan shook the room as he followed her over. A few seconds of silence passed, with him still inside her, the intensity not something she could easily shake off. But she knew where things stood this time.

When Beck pulled out and headed for the bathroom, Chloe immediately pushed herself up, grabbing her dress and shoes. With luck she'd be back in her room before he emerged from the bathroom in time for a freak out.

Deciding she'd rather be covered, even for the short walk across the hall, she put her clothes on the bed and picked up his dress shirt. She pulled it on before scooping up her things again and taking steps toward the door.

"Chloe, stop."

His husky voice compelled her to turn, holding her clothes against her chest.

"I want you to stay." His emerald-green eyes stared at her, willing her to believe he meant it.

"I don't think that's a good idea." For so many reasons, the most important being sleeping in his bed or cuddled in his arms would make keeping her emotional distance that much more difficult.

And it wasn't easy as it was.

He obviously heard her, and to his credit, he paused and debated with himself. She could see the war going on behind his eyes, and she knew the minute he made up his mind. Her heart skipped a beat as he walked over, plucked her clothes out of her grasp, and tossed them on top of his jacket on the dresser.

Then he held out his arm and waited for her to take his hand.

She pursed her lips, frustrated at him for making this more difficult when a few days ago all he wanted was for her to leave and sleep across the hall. "We need to keep smart boundaries."

His eyes gleamed with determination. "But we only have a limited time until you move out, so why deny ourselves pleasure?"

He began to lower his arm when she made up her mind, deciding he was right. "This is against my better judgment," she muttered, accepting his invitation by placing her palm in his.

He slid his shirt off her, leaving her naked and feeling extremely vulnerable. And as they climbed back into bed and he pulled her into his arms, she promised herself she wouldn't read more into these moments than he intended. Losing Owen and being a jilted bride had hurt her pride. Even in this short time, she knew, letting herself fall for Beck could cost her her heart.

★ ★ ★

BECK SLEPT WELL and woke up with his arms around a warm female body. It wasn't something he was used to, but he hadn't been able to watch Chloe walk out on him again. Last time he'd driven her away, but he knew her leaving had been her attempt to keep one step ahead of him. Protect herself before he asked her to leave. But he'd been mentally prepared and had given it thought beforehand, and he trusted her to hold up her end of their temporary agreement.

He was going to need her to be strong. Faced with her wearing his shirt, the bottom hitting her thighs, the sleeves too long, and her cleavage visible, all he could think about was how right she looked. In his clothes, in his bedroom, and in his home. They were *both* going to have to be strong.

And he'd have to keep his heart caged in his chest. It shouldn't be hard. He'd become an expert at keeping people at a distance.

Pushing those thoughts out of the way, he focused on the present and proceeded to wake Chloe by going down on her, something he thoroughly enjoyed doing.

To her.

And followed that up with a slower sex session than last night. Now she lay beside him in his bed. They planned to get up soon, but he was content right where he was. She'd pulled her phone from her purse and was scrolling through while he did the same, making sure no work emergencies had cropped up.

She groaned and he turned his head toward her. "What's wrong?"

A frown etched her face. "This." She shifted the screen of her cell toward him, revealing a photo of her ex-fiancé smiling beside a brown-haired woman with her arms around him, pressing a kiss to his cheek.

"And this." She took the phone back, swiped, and showed him a different picture of them standing hand in hand, looking into each other's eyes. "Rude," she muttered.

"Agreed." Owen's new woman looked like she could use a good meal, and Chloe's ex had no shame. He'd just been a no-show at his own wedding, stood up a woman he'd supposedly cared about, and was now out and about like he'd done nothing wrong. "Why don't you unfollow him and save yourself the aggravation?"

She lifted her shoulder in a dainty shrug. "I asked myself that the other day. Call it morbid curiosity. Like when you pass a crash and can't help looking?"

He chuckled, taking her phone and doing the unfollow for her. "There. He's gone where he should be. Out of sight, out of mind," he said, handing back her cell. He didn't want her to have to look at that asshole ever again.

She treated him to a smile. "Thank you. Considering I have to spend a day at my mom's, writing notes to people who came and brought gifts, and to those who sent engagement presents, so we can send them all back, seeing Owen carefree just pisses me off." Her mother had even offered to handle getting the ring back to Owen and for that Chloe was grateful.

"And I don't blame you, but you need to focus on the fact that you're moving forward and doing things you wouldn't have tried if you were still with him. Then you can remind yourself you dodged a bullet."

Because the vibrant woman inside her had nothing in common with the boring tax attorney who wouldn't have supported her dreams. "Thanks to him, you're becoming who you were meant to be." And she was accomplishing it in record time.

She leaned over and pressed a kiss on his cheek.

"What was that for?" he asked, taken off guard.

"For being sweet. And supportive."

The last thing he thought of himself as was sweet. Supportive? He supposed. Still, he wasn't sure how to reply, but his phone rang, saving him from getting into an emotional discussion.

He picked his cell up from where it lay on the bed and saw his mother was calling. He swiped and answered. "Hi, Mom."

"Hi, honey."

"Is everything okay?"

Beside him, Chloe slid out of bed, walked to the dresser, and began to pull on his shirt.

"Hang on, Mom." He glanced at Chloe. "Where are you going?"

She met his gaze. "I'm going to give you some privacy and go get showered and dressed for the day."

He nodded and returned to his call. "Sorry. What's going on? Is Dad okay?"

"Your father's fine. Stop worrying. Is that the woman Tripp told me is staying with you?" his mom asked.

Beck leaned back against the pillow and winced. His brothers were like gossipy women sometimes. "Yes. I'm helping her out during a rough time."

"That's so sweet. I was calling to make sure you were coming for dinner tonight. Your brothers are going to a Yankees game and won't make it."

"Yeah. They asked me for tickets." They knew he had connections with people in the front office. They'd invited him but he wasn't in the mood to sit at a game. "Of course I'll be there." He wouldn't miss spending as much time with his parents as he could.

"Wonderful. Bring your *girl* friend." She separated the words, but he shook his head at the implication anyway.

He swallowed a groan. "Mom, I don't think–"

"Oh, come on. If she's going through a rough patch, I'm sure she would enjoy getting out of your loft, nice as it is. And having company means you won't be all gloom and doom. I'm determined to remain hopeful about your father, and I insist you do as well."

"Of course, Mom. You know I'll do anything for you." And he meant it.

"Great! I'll add a seat for dinner. I'll see you around six?"

"See you at six." He disconnected the call and glanced up at the ceiling. He was bringing Chloe to his parents' house, and his mother would figure out in a heartbeat they were more than friends. When it came to her kids, she had a sixth sense about those things, and nothing would make her happier than one of her sons settling down.

No matter what said son wanted or had planned.

★ ★ ★

CHLOE WISHED SHE'D had more warning about going to Beck's parents' house for dinner. Like a year would have helped. Though she wasn't sure why, her nerves were on full display. She'd managed to run out and pick up a key lime meringue pie from Petee's Pies on Delancey Street so she wouldn't walk in empty-handed.

"Are you sure your parents want an extra person tonight? When they're going through so much?" Chloe asked the question for what had to be the third time on the drive to his parents' place in Great Neck.

A sexy grin lifted the edges of his mouth as he drove. His sunglasses only added to his appeal. "I swear to you, my mother extended the invitation herself. No prodding from me."

"Does that mean *you* don't want me there?" She didn't have to be perceptive to notice he was tense, too.

He shook his head. "Of course not. I'm just worried about my dad, and I know they are going to put on a good front … like everything is fine and will be fine." He clenched his jaw, then said, "I've been through it before with them, you know?"

"And you don't know whether or not to believe them this time?" She wanted to touch him, to cover his hand with hers and let him know he wasn't alone, but he gripped the wheel tight and clearly wanted his distance.

"I don't know your parents, but you're an adult and I don't think they'd lie to you." She blew out a breath. "Did they lie about Whitney? Or did things just take an unexpected bad turn?"

She knew he didn't like talking about his sister, but asking was the only way not just for her to find out but to help him through things now.

He flipped on the right turn signal and took the exit. "I don't believe they lied. Maybe they're more optimistic than me but I don't understand how. Not after what happened to Whitney."

"I get it. But anything they did or said was because they love you." She hesitated and then dove into the deep end. For Beck because she cared about him. She knew her past had not been as tragic as his, but she could draw some kind of parallel in the hopes of making him think about how he viewed life.

"My parents are nothing like yours." She bit the inside of her cheek. "Don't get me wrong, my mom loves me, but she lived her life in denial so she didn't have to rock the boat of her marriage. Oh, she says she stayed for the kids, but let's face it. How happy are the kids living in a house where the husband is cheating and it's a known issue as we all grew up? I know it's not the same as losing a sibling."

She paused and drew a deep breath. "But what I'm trying to say is that the love you guys have for each other is strong but so is the respect." Respect her family hadn't had for one another. Her parents, anyway. "Trust your parents to tell you the truth and gain strength from their optimism."

His hands curled around the wheel, his knuckles turning white. "That's easy to say but harder to do when I was given every reason to believe Whitney would survive only to lose her despite the positive outlook."

She closed her eyes and sighed. He was a stubborn man with a very valid point, and she didn't know how else to get through to him.

"But Chloe?" He turned toward her before looking back at the road.

"Hmm?"

He reached over and placed his hand over hers. "I appreciate you telling me about your parents, and I know you're just trying to help."

She was. Too bad it wouldn't help him open his heart any time in the near future.

He turned into a driveway of a large colonial-style home in a modern neighborhood that looked fairly new. Since Beck had grown up in the Bronx, she knew this home was one he and his brothers must have helped them buy. The Daniels brothers were good men.

Beck cut the engine. "Ready?"

She picked up the pie from the floor in front of her. Her purse was already hooked on her arm and she met his gaze. "Let's do this."

He winked at her, causing her stomach to tumble over. He'd probably meant to calm her. He'd just reminded her of how easily she was falling for him instead. Shoving that thought out of her head, she climbed out of the car, letting him help her, and followed him up the path to meet his parents.

His mom, a pretty woman with wavy light brown hair and Beck's green eyes, greeted them at the door. Introductions were made while his mother fawned over her son. She led them into the house, which had a modern décor, and they ended up in the kitchen, also modern with gorgeous stainless steel appliances.

She took the pie out of Chloe's hands and put it on the counter and proceeded to pull her into a hug. "I'm so glad you could join us."

A loud sound of a man clearing his throat startled Chloe, and she spun to see a handsome man, an older version of Beck, studying her intently. "I'm Kurt Daniels," he said.

"This is Chloe, Dad."

He nodded, his gaze zeroed in on her face.

"Kurt, stop staring. You're being rude," his mom, who'd insisted Chloe call her Audrey, said to her husband.

He shrugged, not looking sorry. "It's just that she looks familiar," he said. "You said your name's Chloe, right?"

She nodded. "Chloe Kingston."

Audrey's eyes opened wide. "Are you Linc Kingston's sister?"

Chloe nodded. Beside her, Beck stiffened.

"I remember him from your college years," she said to Beck. "You were roommates, and then at some point, you stopped mentioning him."

"Things happened," Beck muttered. "Dad, want to go watch some television?" He was obviously eager to change the subject.

Chloe was still in the dark about her brother and Beck's history, something she intended to change as soon as she had time alone with Linc, and it was time for her to do just that.

Suddenly Kurt snapped his fingers. "I know why you look familiar to me. You're the jilted bride! TMZ and Page Six had photos."

Chloe felt her face begin to flush and grow hot. Though she'd known those articles existed, she hadn't thought people would pay much attention, let alone recognize her.

"Dad!" Beck shot his father an annoyed look.

"I'm sorry, honey." Audrey glanced at Chloe. "Kurt's retirement has given him too much free time to pay attention to gossip on the internet." She shook her head in dismay.

Chloe sighed. There was no way to avoid the truth. "That's me. Beck helped me that first night, and he's been my savior ever since." She smiled up at him. "You raised a gentleman, Mrs.…" At the other woman's scowl Chloe corrected herself. "I mean Audrey."

"I didn't mean to upset you," Kurt said. "My wife is right. I spend way too much time surfing the internet and watching trash on TV. A part of me misses my job but my back won't let me work anymore." He placed a hand on his lower back and rubbed the area.

"What did you do before you retired?" Chloe asked. Beck had never said.

"I was a building inspector for the city," he said, obviously proud of his occupation.

"Sounds interesting." Before she could ask another question, Beck announced he and his father were going into the family room, but not before shooting Chloe a questioning look.

Was she okay? She could read his mind and offered him a nod and a smile.

She was great, as were his parents.

She and Audrey ended up in the kitchen. Dinner was already made, the table set, and all Chloe could do was sit on a stool by the counter and talk to Beck's mom, though she had offered to help.

"So … you and my son." Apparently Audrey was direct, which Chloe admired.

"We're good friends. Like I said, he rescued me the night of my non-wedding and has been giving me a place to stay while I get back on my feet. He's been very generous." And that's all a parent needed to know.

Audrey picked up the salad bowl and removed the foil covering the top. "That's interesting because I've never known him to step up for a stranger. And even if he felt compelled to help you out the night of the wedding, having you move in? It's not his typical personality, if you know what I mean."

Chloe narrowed her gaze. "If you're afraid I'm taking advantage of your son, I can assure you I'm not. I–" Before she could inform his mother she was helping with cooking and cleaning and doing whatever else she could around the loft, Audrey shook her head and rushed over.

"God, no. I didn't mean it like that. Just the opposite, in fact. I'm telling you if my son is helping you out, he cares." Audrey beamed at her observation.

She obviously wanted her son settled and happy and had no idea Beck had other plans.

It wasn't Chloe's place to tell his mother things about Beck he hadn't explained himself. "As I mentioned, we're good friends."

"Well, Beck doesn't have many of those, and he's never moved a woman in before." She rushed over to the refrigerator and opened the door. "Do you like creamy Italian dressing?" Audrey asked. "I also have vinaigrette, French…"

Head spinning, Chloe replied, "Creamy Italian is fine, thank you." She opted to ignore his mother's other comment. And since she didn't mention her husband's diagnosis or problems, Chloe didn't either.

But in the few minutes she'd had with Beck's mother, Chloe had a few observations. His mom was a bulldog, which showed Chloe where Beck got his determination in business to go after what he wanted. It explained how he was so successful so fast and all on his own.

She also tended to ignore the important things and push them aside like they weren't happening … her husband's illness, for example. And Chloe had no doubt if asked, Audrey would assure her that Kurt would be fine. She wouldn't want to hear otherwise. Which explained why Beck was so frustrated and why he had a hard time deciphering truth from blind hope.

Audrey meant well, but she didn't want to see the reality in front of her, and she had the definite impression Kurt followed his wife's lead in all things.

Then there was Beck. He wasn't just more of a realist, he was a glass-half-empty kind of guy. That way, if the worst happened, he'd protected himself ahead of time.

Now that Chloe knew the forces that had shaped him, she was even more convinced there'd be no changing his mind once he'd made a decision. He'd put Chloe outside his inner circle, and that's where she would remain.

★ ★ ★

"YOUR PARENTS ARE amazing," Chloe said as they headed back to the city.

Beck couldn't help but grin. "I'm partial to them myself. And they liked you a lot." He could tell they'd fallen in love with Chloe immediately.

He'd known it by the gleam in his mom's eye and the way she'd grinned at him when Chloe wasn't looking. His father merely patted him on the back as if he'd done something good by bringing her over. That was his dad's seal of approval. It helped that Chloe was the perfect guest, bringing dessert and offering to help in the kitchen, which gave his mother a chance to grill her about her life.

"I'm glad." She stretched her legs out in front of her and groaned, the sound going straight to his cock. "I noticed your parents changed the subject every time you tried to bring up your father's surgery."

He set his jaw. "Yeah." Beck had gritted his teeth and gotten through it. "I just have to wait until he's operated on and we have results." And that was all the discussion he wanted to have on the subject. "So … do you have plans for tomorrow?"

He couldn't imagine her sitting around the house and staring at the walls or the television.

She shook her head. "Not really. I could go back to work with Linc until I hear about the contest or find something else. In fact, I probably should." But her pout told him how she felt about that.

He looked back at the road. "I have a better idea. Come to the office with me. There's someone I want you to meet."

She pivoted toward him. "Who?" she asked, excitement in her voice.

"My in-house designer, Natasha." He had a feeling she and Chloe would get along, and maybe Natasha could help Chloe find direction.

"I'd love that. Thank you."

"You're welcome."

She shifted in the passenger seat. "Umm, there's something else. I told my friend Amelia, the Realtor, to set up a couple of appointments for me to see the apartments I thought might be possibilities."

He'd forgotten about her intention to move. More like he'd pushed it out of his head.

"I'll go with you." The least he could do was make sure she ended up in a good place, though he had feeling her brother would be all over her choice.

"You really don't have to do that," she said of his offer.

"Well, I want to." He gripped the wheel tighter in his hand.

She shrugged. "Okay then. I'll keep you posted on the day and time."

After that, they fell into silence until they reached his loft. The moment he stepped inside, awareness of their situation settled on his shoulders. He was living with the same woman he was currently sleeping with. Would she expect to be in his bed every night? Was that even what he wanted?

He'd enjoyed sleeping with her last night and waking up with her this morning, both solid reasons to make sure it didn't become a habit. The biggest thing he needed to worry about tonight was not insulting Chloe when he went into his bedroom alone.

Beck was tense as he locked up and they headed down the hall to the bedrooms, and he paused at his door, prepared to let her down gently. But she made a left and stepped into her room.

"Beck?" she asked, turning in the doorway and facing him.

"Yes?" He waited for her to tell him she'd change and come in. Or wash up and meet him in his room.

"Thank you for tonight. I enjoyed meeting your family," she said, treating him to a genuine smile.

"Good night, Beck."

Still smiling, or maybe it was more like a grin, she stepped back and shut her door, closing him and his arrogant assumptions out.

★ ★ ★

CHLOE LEANED AGAINST the door and breathed out a huge sigh, aware of Beck on the other side, probably shocked. From the moment they'd entered the loft, Beck had been obviously uptight. And since where she'd be sleeping tonight was on her mind, she'd taken one look at him and guessed it was on his, too.

Beck the businessman would hate how well she'd read him. He hadn't wanted her in his bed and she knew why. He didn't want to set a precedent that would let her get closer to him, even if it meant they'd have great sex if he gave in to desire and not his fears.

They'd both be sleeping alone tonight. She could only hope she'd made her point. Points, actually. She wasn't clingy, she could take a hint, and she had her pride.

Once alone in his bed, maybe he'd realize he'd made a mistake. A girl could hope. With a sigh, she pushed herself off the door and headed to her bathroom to wash up and undress.

Chapter Nine

BECK WOKE UP alone with morning wood and a bad attitude. He'd climbed into bed by himself, exactly the way he'd wanted it, but he wasn't satisfied with the way things had ended last night with Chloe. And he had only himself to blame. He desired her and he didn't want to let himself have her.

Frustrated, he tossed off the covers and headed for the shower, meeting up with Chloe in the kitchen. She was dressed in a pair of black leggings and high-heeled short boots with one of the man-styled shirts she favored, this one in pink, and it reminded him of her wearing his dress shirt the other day. She'd looked vulnerable and sexy and so fucking appealing at the same time.

One hip propped against the counter, she drank her coffee, and there was another one waiting for him.

She picked up the mug and held it out. "Morning!" she said cheerfully.

"If you say so," he muttered, taking a long sip and hoping the caffeine improved his mood.

"Sleep well?" she asked, a teasing glint in her eyes.

He narrowed his gaze. Had she tested him last night, going into her room alone just to see if he'd invite her in? She was definitely smart enough to know that he'd been unsure about how to handle their sleeping arrangements, and she'd taken control of the situation. And probably knew he'd regret letting her slip away.

"Drink your coffee. It seems like you need it," she said, a grin on her pretty face.

Yeah, she'd known what she was doing. But it wasn't coffee he desired. Drawing a deep breath, he reminded himself he was through with the internal bullshit and could have her if he wanted her. And he did.

He stepped close, took the mug out of her hand, and placed it on the granite beside her phone. Grabbing her by the hips, he pulled her flush against him until his cock settled between her thighs.

"What are you doing?" she asked in a trembling voice.

"Making up for what I missed out on last night," he said and brought his mouth down on hers.

She immediately wound her arms around his neck and kissed him back, eagerly accepting him as he thrust his tongue past her lips. He tasted her sweetness, and every reason not to be with her fled in the wake of their incredible connection.

He ran his hands down her back and cupped her ass, and she moaned as her sex rubbed hard against his erection. So much for work. He'd much rather make time for this, he thought, when the ring of her cell interrupted them.

She lifted her head. "Ignore it."

She didn't have to say so twice. He dipped his head and recaptured her lips. Their teeth clashed and their tongues tangled … and her damned phone rang again.

"Ugh. I'd better see who's looking for me." She pushed herself away from him and turned toward her cell. "It's Linc."

Shooting Beck an apologetic glance, she answered the call. "Is everything okay?" she asked in place of the standard *hello*.

Beck drew a deep breath and adjusted himself in his pants, but he definitely listened to her end of the conversation.

"No, I didn't see Page Six. Why?" she asked.

Beck narrowed his gaze, immediately taking out his phone and looking up the site online.

"We were going for dinner, and I didn't see anyone take a picture of us." Chloe met Beck's gaze, but he'd already found the photo and headline.

Jilted Bride Moves On? The photo below was a picture of Beck helping Chloe out of the limousine outside the hotel, but they were definitely staring into each other's eyes. And though he hadn't seen anyone using their phones to take a photo either, obviously someone had. Since the club was located on the top floor of a hotel, of course there had been people walking around outside.

"Hang on. I'll look," she said.

Knowing he had no choice, Beck turned the screen toward her.

She closed her eyes and sighed. "I just saw it," she said to Linc. "Ignore it. I plan to." She listened and her eyes opened wide. "What? I'm going to pretend you didn't say that, and I can't believe you care what people think!" she said, raising her voice.

What the fuck was Linc's problem now? Beck wondered.

"Well, that's what it sounded like. It's my life and I'll see who I want, when I want, and live where I want."

Beck wanted to applaud her for standing her ground.

"You want me to meet you for lunch?" Chloe asked her brother. "After you just gave me a hard time?" She rolled her eyes. "Okay, yes. Fine. Where?" She paused. "Ocean Prime? Are you trying to wine and dine me, big brother?"

Beck waited not so patiently to hear why Linc was giving his sister shit now, ignoring the pit in his stomach from wishing he had a sister to care for, take for lunch, and worry about the way Linc did Chloe.

She grinned. "One o'clock is fine. And yes, I know you love me, but can you take a step back before you come at me? I can handle things." She must have liked what she heard because she said, "Love you, too, and see you later," before disconnecting the call.

She glanced at him with a wary expression on her face.

"What's wrong?" he asked.

She dampened her lower lip. "Well, the article mentions you by name, for one thing. It talks about how I'm moving onward and upward to bigger and better things." She winced at that. "I can't imagine you're happy with the publicity."

"I appreciate you worrying about me but it's fine. I've been mentioned a time or two before." It came with his fast rise to the top of the New York real estate market and the money he made. "But that wasn't what had your brother worked up, was it?"

He folded his arms across his chest, defensive without even knowing what Linc had said.

"He was upset about the photo," she admitted. "He said that I just got out of one relationship and I was jumping into another and what did I think I was doing? I needed time … blah, blah, blah." She made a hand motion with her fingers, imitating her brother's mouth moving.

Beck narrowed his gaze. "That wasn't all he said. He has to be pissed that it was me you were photographed with."

She nodded slowly. "He thought we were just friends and asked how could I think it was a good idea to be with you when I knew you two had issues. Even if I don't know what they are," she muttered under her breath. "But you'd better believe I'm going to find out at lunch today."

"Is that why you let him off the hook so easily and agreed to meet him?" Beck asked.

She nodded. "I want to understand this crazy dynamic and you're not talking." She waited a beat, obviously hoping he'd clue her in.

"Sorry, princess." It really wasn't his place to air Linc's dirty laundry and change how she thought of her brother. It remained to be seen what Linc would say and how much truth he'd tell.

"Are you ready to go to the office?" he asked.

She nodded. "Just let me grab my bag and laptop."

As much as he'd like to pick up where they'd left off when they'd been interrupted, the mood had been broken. But he'd learned something last night, and he wasn't going to waste another night alone in his bed when he could take advantage of whatever time they had left until she moved out.

★ ★ ★

CHLOE WAITED FOR Linc at the restaurant. The hostess had seated her at his favorite table, and she settled in, ordering a club soda with lime while she waited. The space was huge and not solely a seafood restaurant as the name implied. Also known for its steaks, Ocean Prime boasted a chic atmosphere with brass circular overhead fixtures and a dark motif inside. Chloe couldn't help analyzing the décor. It was second nature for her to study a place's interior design.

She'd had a couple of hours at Beck's office, meeting his friend and in-house designer, Natasha Banks, who had been thrilled to have Chloe around. They knew of one another through the industry and had talked shop for the better part of the morning.

When she'd gone to Beck's office to let him know she was leaving for lunch, she'd noticed immediately his mood had turned. He'd informed her that his mother had called and his father's surgery was scheduled for Thursday morning. Chloe had let Beck know she'd be there holding his hand, whether he wanted her there or not. He'd been there for her and she intended to repay the favor.

"Sorry I'm late." Linc interrupted her thoughts, joining her at the table. He walked over and kissed her cheek before taking a chair across from her.

"It's fine. I haven't been here long." She took in

her brother's relaxed face and smiled. "Almost-married life agrees with you," she said. "So when will you and Jordan tie the knot?"

He shrugged, putting the menu aside. No doubt he already knew what he wanted. "We have to figure out timing. Neither one of us wants a big event, but Mom will kill me if we elope. Not to mention Jordan's mother." He semi-fake shuddered.

Jordan's mother was a strong woman who'd been their housekeeper for years. She was no-nonsense, loving, and Linc was right. She wouldn't tolerate not being there for her daughter's wedding.

Chloe leaned forward in her chair. "I know you held off because my wedding was planned. Please don't do it again because you're worried about my feelings. I'm fine," she assured him. "So get yourselves married before the baby is born."

He nodded. "I hear you and thanks."

The waiter came over and took their orders, an ahi tuna salad for Chloe and cheeseburger for Linc. After the server took their menus, she met her brother's gaze.

"We need to talk," she said.

He nodded. "I know. I've been high-handed and difficult, but you don't understand why."

At least he'd given her an opening to ask. "Then tell me, Linc. Why do you hate Beck so much? And why won't he explain anything to me about his past with you?" she asked.

Her brother's eyes opened wide. "You asked him directly and he refused to tell you?"

She nodded. "He said something about it not being his place and not wanting to change how I saw you. So I'm here and I'm asking you to tell me yourself."

He drew in a deep breath, and she could see how difficult this was for him, making her wonder just what both men were hiding.

"Okay, look, I'm going to sum it up, but it isn't pretty and he's right. You won't look at me the same way after you hear it."

"Linc, you're my brother. There's nothing you can say that will change how I feel about you."

He gestured for the waiter, who walked over. "I changed my mind. Can I get a Macallan on the rocks?" he asked, and when the server was gone, Linc met Chloe's gaze. "Beck and I were roommates freshman year. We both had girlfriends and the four of us hung out together."

She opened her mouth to tell him she remembered Lacey, but he held up a hand, and she understood he just wanted to get the story out. So she sat forward and waited as he continued.

"One night, Lacey went home for the weekend,

and I was at a frat party. I was so drunk I barely remember how I got home. Beck was working a late shift like he usually did because he needed money to pay for things at school. And his girlfriend, Jenna, resented the times he couldn't go out." Linc ran a hand through his hair, more upset than Chloe was used to seeing him. "Like I said, I don't recall much but I woke up to Beck coming into the room. I was naked and so was Jenna, beside me in bed."

"Oh, shit."

He nodded somberly. "I kind of remember a woman crawling into bed and telling me she was back. I swear to God I thought it was Lacey. You know how I feel about Dad and his cheating. I'd never do it intentionally. But it happened anyway because Jenna wanted his attention. And boy, did she get it."

Just not the way she'd wanted, Chloe was sure, and she swallowed hard.

"Are you certain you two …?"

He nodded. "I found a condom wrapper on the floor." He shook his head. "At least she thought ahead and made sure she couldn't get pregnant," he said, not meeting her gaze.

Chloe sighed. "Beck must have been hurt," she said softly. "And you? That bitch used you! Couldn't Beck see that?"

Linc shook his head. "Not at the time, and wit

the way things have been between us all these years, he probably still hasn't forgiven me. In the meantime, he's undercut me on deals since we've been in business. And right before Dad died, he approached Beck with a land deal. Dad, with his dementia, put up a piece of the company if he didn't come up with the money."

Chloe's hands shook, and she put her drink, which she'd just picked up, back down on the table. "What?"

"As you can imagine, I was in a hell of a position after Dad died and Beck, the asshole, didn't make it easy on me. So there's a lot of bad blood." Linc leaned forward, arms on the table. "Now can you see why I'm worried he's using you to get back at me?" he asked just as the waiter put down his scotch.

Chloe processed while Linc was served his drink. Once they were alone, she took a sip of her club soda. "I'm sorry you and Beck were taken in by a girl with an agenda and lost years of friendship. I'm really sorry she used you the way she did." She frowned, wanting to strangle the woman for what amounted to having nonconsensual sex with Chloe's brother. But she wouldn't make Linc uncomfortable by pointing that out.

"But as for Beck and Dad…" She glanced at the table before looking up again. "I can't imagine Beck deliberately using Dad. Did Beck know Dad was sick?

Because we agreed to keep it quiet."

Dipping his head, Linc groaned. "To his credit, he didn't."

"And he wouldn't use me, either." Of that Chloe was certain. "We have a genuine friendship. He was there the night Owen dumped me–"

"Which you wouldn't let your family do," Linc reminded her.

She ignored that bit of truth. "I didn't want anyone's pity." And she'd needed to be alone to process things. "And Beck was there when I was depressed. He even came to you to help me out. And he encouraged me to follow my dreams," she said, her voice rising. Catching herself, she lowered her voice. "Does that sound like a man with an agenda?"

"Lunch," the waiter said, approaching them with plates in his hand.

He served them while Chloe and Linc silently watched. She was waiting for them to be alone before she finished this private conversation.

Once her ahi tuna was in front of her and Linc had his burger, she glanced at him. "I need you to answer me."

"No. It sounds like Beck cares about you," Linc said, and she knew what that admission cost him. "One more thing. I know I've said it a million times, but let me say it once more. I just want what's best for you." He drew a deep breath. "And if that's Beck, I'll deal. I'll do what I can to make things right with him. For you."

A lump rose to Chloe's throat. Pushing her chair back, she walked to Linc's side of the table and wrapped her arms around his neck. "Thank you. I love you, Linc. And your being willing to do that for me means everything."

He hugged her back. "I love you, too."

She sat back down and picked up her fork. "The thing is, you're not going to have to accept Beck in my life long-term. He has no intention of ever falling in love or getting married. Not that I'm thinking of marriage," she rushed to assure Linc. "But what we have is temporary. After that, time will tell if we can remain friends."

Linc studied her in silence for so long she squirmed in her seat. "What?" she asked him.

"His sister died when he was eighteen, right before he left for college. I know that fucked with his head. It was just another reason he didn't give Jenna what she wanted back then, although I doubt he realized it at the time."

She nodded. "That's the problem. He's holding on to his pain, not willing to let anyone get close except the family he already has."

"Seems to me you've already gotten that close."

Linc picked up his burger. "Are you going to let him push you away?"

"Oh, my God, Linc, are you really trying to convince me to keep Beck in my life?" She opened and closed her mouth in complete shock.

A grin lifted his lips. "I promised Jordan I'd get over myself and stop being an ass. On the ride here, I realized she was right. I want you to be happy." He shrugged. "Now let's eat. We can talk more over dessert."

After the long discussion with Linc and the reminder of how little Beck wanted from her, Chloe barely tasted her salad. She did, however, indulge in an after-lunch dessert drink, a Salty Caramel, consisting of Ketel One, caramel, cream, and Madagascar vanilla cream.

In the end, Linc didn't push for more conversation, and she was grateful. She'd gotten what she needed from her brother, his support, and acceptance, of a relationship with Beck. Linc bent for her and she loved him for it.

The question remained, could she get Beck to bend, too? Time would tell.

Chapter Ten

THE NIGHT AFTER Chloe's lunch with her brother, she'd opened up to Beck over dinner. According to Chloe, Linc had told her everything about his falling-out with Beck, without minimizing the fact that he'd slept with Beck's girlfriend. Chloe had defended him, mentioning how proud she was that he'd accepted his role in the breakup of their friendship.

As much as it galled him, Beck appreciated the man's candor and acceptance of responsibility. Linc had also revealed Beck's role in the business deal with their father, but when Chloe had asked her brother if Beck had known their father had dementia at the time, Linc admitted Beck hadn't been aware. It had been a transaction, pure and simple. With a little satisfaction on Beck's end thrown in, but Chloe didn't seem to hold that against him.

Although Linc still wasn't happy about his sister's friendship with Beck, apparently he'd promised to find a way to deal with it in a better way. Another point for her Linc Kingston. Despite his personal feelings, which Beck had to admit had diminished since seeing how much Linc cared for his sister, Beck was grateful he hadn't given Chloe a hard time. And since Beck didn't have to deal with Linc personally, all was well.

For the rest of the week, the specter of his father's surgery hovered, and he kept busy with work. Since Chloe had moved in, he'd been neglecting the hands-on part of the business, and though his higher-up people could handle it, he'd spent the time catching up. He was aware of the fact that he'd stopped paying as much attention to Chloe and transferred his focus to his business, but it was necessary on many levels.

Work needed him.

His family needed him.

And Chloe shouldn't get used to his complete attention.

That didn't mean he ignored her at night, and she seemed to accept and maybe even understand the withdrawal that was obvious to both of them. Beck needed space while he dealt with the upcoming surgery and whatever the results might be, and Chloe gave it to him. She also provided warmth and caring in bed.

Selfish as he was, he accepted what she offered. How could he not when it was given so freely?

On Wednesday morning, Chloe and Beck walked into his private office as her cell phone rang, and she answered immediately. "Hi. What's up?"

Beck sat down behind the desk and waited for h

to finish.

"Thanks, Amelia. Yes! I'll see you at three. Text me the first address." As usual, Chloe's smile kicked him in the gut. She was so damned beautiful, and he was drawn to her no matter what else was happening in his life.

"Thanks!" She disconnected the call and glanced up, meeting Beck's gaze.

"Amelia. That's your Realtor friend, right?" As he asked, his stomach twisted, and he breathed through the uncomfortable sensation.

She nodded. "She was able to schedule three apartment viewings today. The ones I liked best. Two of the buildings are close to each other, so it's not hard to see them all this afternoon."

He studied her face but couldn't get a read on her feelings about how fast things were potentially happening with her move. He, on the other hand, hated the building pressure in his gut.

He put his hand on the mouse, turning on his computer, and glanced at today's schedule on the screen. "I'll reschedule a call and I can go with you." He wanted to make sure these were suitable places for her.

"I already told you that you don't have to come with me."

He narrowed his gaze. "I'm going."

His tone had her widening her eyes. "Okay. Thank you."

He nodded. "Where are the buildings located?" Hopefully downtown, somewhere close by so he could meet her for lunch on occasion.

"Two on the Upper East Side and one in Midtown," she said. "Okay, I'm going to Natasha's office. I'll stop by at two thirty when I'm ready to leave." With a wave, she walked out the door, leaving him staring at her sexy ass swaying as she walked.

Pushing away the locations that took her from him, Beck got to work, and anyone who called got the brunt of his mood. Until Ronnie, who'd been working for him for three years and wasn't afraid of him, snapped back and let him know he was being a dick to the people he worked with. Not in those words.

But Beck knew she was right. Still, he had to deal with Chloe leaving soon, and deep down, he knew the separation was necessary for them both.

★ ★ ★

CHLOE WISHED BECK hadn't joined her. His mood was atrocious, and she understood he was anxious about his dad's surgery tomorrow. Based on how often he'd holed up in his office this week, he had much better things to do than go apartment hunting with her. Leaving him would be hard enough, and she needed the space to evaluate these apartments without his negative energy infusing every unit and individual room they went into.

They started on the Upper East Side. The first apartment he deemed too small and, since it had no pets, something they hadn't put in the listing, and one day she might want a dog, she didn't argue.

The second one was two bedrooms and one and a half baths in a doorman building.

Beck stepped past Amelia, strode from bedroom to bedroom, and folded his arms across his chest. "This won't work. If you have a guest, they'll have to share your bathroom." Beck waved a hand, dismissing the place, and she hadn't even examined the kitchen or seen the view.

Ignoring him, she walked through the apartment and over to the window. "Look at this." The unit was on the twenty-third floor and overlooked the East River.

Beck grunted from behind her.

She took in the kitchen next and loved the dark granite countertops, white cabinets, and stainless appliances. "This is pretty."

"The whole place is too small," he said.

Chloe turned to see Amelia glancing from Chloe to Beck, taking a step back when her gaze landed on his frown. "I'll just leave you two to discuss things," she murmured and walked out into the hall.

"You're in a horrible mood and I understand why. You're worried about tomorrow. I get it. But I'm the one who has to choose," she reminded him.

He raised an eyebrow. "Did the last apartment or this one appeal to you?"

"Well, no, but I wanted to look at them and make a decision."

He shook his head, a wry smile lifting those smoldering lips.

"Okay, fine. You're right. But give me a chance to say it first," she said, grinning back. "It's my life and I need to be in control."

He nodded in understanding. "Okay. I get it. But I hope the next one is much bigger or we're going to have a problem," he muttered.

Rolling her eyes, she stepped past him and headed to Amelia to give her the final verdict on apartment number two.

The third place was amazing. Modern and not quite ten years old, the condo was a duplex, much bigger, as Beck had demanded, with two bedrooms down four steps, the master on the main level, a beautifully sized living room, state-of-the-art kitchen, and a view of a park. Chloe felt like she had a keeper.

"I love it!"

Amelia nodded. "I thought you would. It's a condominium, though, so you need to jump through some hoops and get approved. But first we start with an offer. If you're ready that quickly."

"I'm sure she needs to see some other places." Beck spoke up for the first time in this building.

To his credit, he'd allowed her the space she'd needed, from meeting the doorman to discussing amenities and walking through the apartment itself.

"Actually, I don't. I did research on all the places I looked at, and this one is perfect. This apartment is the only one available, and no others seem to be coming up any time soon." She turned to Beck.

If he didn't want her to move out, if he wanted her to stay, this was the time for him to speak up, and she wasn't referring to him complaining about the apartment itself.

She waited a beat and waited some more. When he didn't say anything, she ignored the scowl on his face and named a number to offer the condo owner.

"That's a solid price, and the owner will like it even if he does come back with a counter," Amelia said. "There's also a chance that the condo owner may want to sell. Would you be interested in buying outright?"

"Hang on. You need to do a lot more research before you agree to buy something," Beck said.

She set her jaw. "Do you think I don't know that? My family is in real estate. I'll get back to you," she told the agent.

Amelia nodded in understanding. "It's just something he mentioned to me when I told him I had a showing today. Let's keep in touch, and I'll talk to him about the rental in the meantime." She smiled at Chloe and ignored Beck.

"Sounds great," Chloe said.

They stepped into the hall and Amelia locked the apartment. All three of them took an elevator downstairs before Chloe and Beck parted ways with the real estate agent on the street.

Turning to Beck, Chloe opened her mouth to yell at him for his attitude, but he stopped her by bringing his mouth down on hers, his tongue sliding through her lips and tangling with hers. As usual, her body melted into him, her brain short-circuiting thanks to his kiss.

He lifted his head and met her gaze. "I didn't mean to undercut or underestimate you. I'm just stressed and overwhelmed worrying about tomorrow."

Her anger fled with his sort-of apology and she sighed. "I know. Trust me, I'm not going to throw away millions on an apartment I don't know enough about." Millions she had thanks to a trust fund set up by her father's father.

"I know. I was looking out for you." He put a hand on her back and flagged down a taxi and was silent during the ride back to his loft downtown.

★ ★ ★

CHLOE LAY IN Beck's bed. After they'd had an amazing, satisfying round of sex, he'd pulled her into his arms and fallen into a deep sleep. This whole week, she'd accepted that he'd been using her to exorcise the demons that haunted him. *Used* wasn't the right word. It wasn't that any body in bed would do. She knew he wanted only her, just as much as she understood it was temporary.

He'd rolled onto his back, releasing her from his hold, and beside her, he slept hard. She was glad he'd been able to fall asleep given tomorrow was his dad's surgery. She, on the other hand, was tossing and turning. His moodiness this past week had been emotionally draining, but instead of crashing like he had, she stared at the ceiling because her mind wouldn't shut off.

She thought back to her lunch with Linc. After their talk, she'd been optimistic about possibilities, and she'd hoped Beck would realize not only did he care about her, he wanted her in his life. And not just on the periphery. After all, when he let down his guard, they had fun, enjoyed meals and the ins and outs of living together, and they were in sync in so many ways. More so than she'd ever been with Owen.

A few weeks ago, she'd been a stranger to Beck, yet he'd stepped up and made her see how much was possible if she'd push past her fear. She'd tried so hard to do the same for him, but he didn't seem to be willing to try and get past his issues.

Linc was just one example. She'd told him about her brother's admission about sleeping with Beck's girlfriend and how he'd known the rift was his fault. Chloe had hoped Beck would soften toward her brother. Instead he'd listened, said he was glad she knew the truth and that Linc would no longer give her a hard time. He'd acted like the story had nothing to do with him at all, because he'd distanced himself so far from the relationship with his one-time friend, he had no interest in any kind of personal détente. And it was sad.

As for Chloe herself, the closer they came to his father's surgery day, the further away from her he pulled. As she watched him sleep, her heart squeezed hard in her chest. This was the only time his expression was soft and relaxed, not tortured. She wanted so much more for him than he seemed willing to accept or give, all because he refused to open his heart to anyone outside his immediate family. Loss. His fears were so real.

She traced a hand down his face and pressed a kiss to his cheek before rolling over, determined to fall asleep.

★ ★ ★

BECK WAS UP early, without the help of an alarm clock, prepared to face the day. Though he'd told Chloe she didn't need to come to the hospital, she'd been up and ready even before he was. They met up with his brothers in the waiting room, where Mom would come once she'd settled their father in.

Time dragged by and even his brothers, who were usually good for jokes and laughs, were silent. Chloe stayed throughout, bringing back coffee and snacks and generally doing whatever she could for his family but mostly for him. And when the surgeon stepped into the waiting room, she grasped his hand and held on tight.

The woman's gaze came to his mother. "Mrs. Daniels?"

Audrey was already on her feet. "Yes, Dr. Skinner. How is he?"

Everyone had stood and waited.

The doctor smiled. "Surgery went well. We were able to go in laparoscopically as we'd hoped. We thought it was stage one, but it appears the cancer has grown through the wall of the colon but not..."

From there, Beck's vision went blurry, and a rush sounded inside his ears. He heard the words *lymph nodes*, *possible chemotherapy*, and *prognosis*, and his world collapsed around him.

"Beck? Did you hear what she said?" his mother asked. "Although it's stage two, they're very hopeful."

"Right. Like they were hopeful with Whitney." The walls were closing in, and he needed to get out of here. "I have to go."

His brothers looked at him with concern on their faces.

"Beck, wait." Chloe stepped up to him. "I'm sure you want to see your father once you're allowed, so let's sit down and we can talk."

He shook his head. He didn't want to break down in front of her or, worse, feel closer to her while she tried to comfort him, an impossible feat at this point in time.

She placed her hand on his arm, and he deliberately shrugged it off, not wanting her concern or her pity. "I need to be alone."

And on that note, he turned and strode out of the room and away from the hospital and the words that reminded him of another time and place, when the outcome hadn't been positive at all.

★ ★ ★

CHLOE WATCHED BECK go and did her best not to take his rejection personally. She'd been watching him while the doctor discussed her findings and had seen him shut down, his expression go blank. The color had drained from his face, and she'd been worried about him even before he spoke.

"Chloe, don't let him get to you. He's not dealing well with Dad's illness because it reminds him of something," Tripp said, obviously not sure how much she knew.

She glanced at the man who'd lost his twin yet still seemed to be more composed than Beck. Everyone processed death differently, and Tripp was a medical professional. He'd had more experience with illness after his sister's passing. Chloe had no doubt Tripp's career choice had everything to do with his twin's illness.

"I'll drive you home, and by the time I get back, maybe I'll be able to see Dad." Drew glanced at her, his warm gaze comforting.

Audrey walked over to her. "Go on, honey. It's going to be a long day, and you've done enough for us already." She patted Chloe's arm. "Thank you for being there for my son. I hope you don't take his reactions too personally. He had the most difficult time processing Whitney's death. I took the boys for counseling, but I honestly don't think Beck really listened or opened up." She lifted her shoulders and sighed.

"You did the best you could," Chloe murmured. "And you were dealing with your own loss. Beck's going to have to figure things out for himself." She had the distinct impression he wasn't going to let her help him, either.

Drew hooked his arm through hers. "Come on."

"Are you sure? I don't mind taking an Uber, and that way you can wait here." She didn't want to put anyone out on an already stressful day.

Beck's brother nodded. "Positive. This way I keep busy instead of sitting around waiting."

She shot him a grateful look and said her good-byes. Both Tripp and Audrey promised to let her know if they heard from Beck, and she hoped he checked in with someone. His family had enough to worry about.

Drew had his car and drove her downtown to Beck's. He insisted on walking her up to the loft and making sure she got inside safely. She assumed he also wanted to see if Beck had just gone home. He hadn't.

"Do you have any idea where he went?" she asked as Drew turned to leave.

He shook his head. "At some point, he'll end up somewhere to grab a drink and brood. I'm going to see Dad, and then Tripp and I will go looking for him. I have a couple of ideas where he'll end up."

She swallowed hard. "Bring him back safely," sh

said, her voice hoarse from trying not to cry.

She was worried and stressed and very concerned about Beck's reaction to something that really did sound potentially positive in the long run. He'd gone somewhere else while that doctor spoke, and Chloe had to wonder if he'd heard everything she said or put his own spin on the words that went in one ear and out another.

"I will, Chloe." Drew pulled her into a hug. "You're good for my brother. I know he's got walls up but don't give up on him, okay?"

She treated him to a small smile. "I'm not sure the final decision of what happens between us is going to be mine. But thank you. I know he's going to need his family. I'm glad you're all so close."

He winked as he headed out, leaving her alone in Beck's apartment with no idea where he'd gone. Having known the day would be long, she was already dressed in comfortable clothes, so she kicked off her shoes and left them by the door, then grabbed her iPad from her room and settled in on the sofa in the family room to wait.

To kill time and avoid worrying, she touched base with her friends who'd been calling her all through the weeks since the wedding, wanting to know how she was doing. She'd let them know she was fine, but now she began to open up about her life and her plans, feeling freer each time she explained leaving her job, entering the contest, and considering opening her own business.

With no news from Beck or his brothers, she pulled out her phone and texted him. Simple questions like *how are you? Where are you? Want me to meet you someplace?* The texts went unread and unanswered.

She'd eaten dinner and fallen asleep on the sofa reading when she heard the sound of the front door of the apartment opening.

"That's it. Come on. Just a few more steps." It sounded like Tripp talking, and Chloe moved the reader from her stomach and stood, rushing over to meet them.

Tripp's arm was around Beck, who leaned against his brother, as Tripp guided him inside. "Bedroom?" Tripp asked Chloe before she could speak.

She nodded, following an obviously drunk Beck as his brother led him to his room and unceremoniously dumped him on the bed.

Chloe frowned and rushed over, lifting his feet, allowing him to stretch out on the mattress. She pulled off his shoes and set them on the floor before turning to Tripp.

"What happened?"

He shrugged. "Drew and I split up. He went to the club and I hit up Club TEN29. I found him shit-faced and about to order another drink. You can see for yourself he'd have ended up on the floor."

She narrowed her gaze. "Where's the club?"

"Not far from here. We know the owners," Tripp said, glancing at Beck, who was on his back and snoring.

She sighed. "I've never seen him drunk."

"He doesn't do it often. Or ever, really. A drink or two to relax and that's it. He's just working off his demons. He'll be fine in the morning." He pulled a cell from his pocket and handed it to her. "This is Beck's. It was on the counter where he was sitting. I grabbed it on the way out."

She nodded, accepting the phone. "I'll make sure he gets it in the morning. Tripp, wait. How's your father?" She asked both for herself and for Beck, who would want to know when he sobered up.

He slid his hands into his back pockets. "Dad's tough. He's doing everything the doctors and nurses tell him, and he's determined to get out of there in a few days. They won't know if he needs chemo until the biopsies come back, but we're hopeful. So are the doctors. Not that my brother heard anything they said." He gestured to Beck, jerking his thumb in his sibling's direction.

Chloe bit the inside of her cheek. "He hasn't gotten over it."

"Whitney," Tripp said, stiffening. "Yeah. I know. We all reacted differently, but Beck's always been a caretaker and he took on that role with my twin. I couldn't handle it but that's my problem. But Beck?" He shook his head. "He needs to stop living based on the past and look to the future. I tried to tell him that tonight, but given his condition, I doubt he heard a damned thing I said."

"I know," she said sadly.

"Hey, are you sure you can take care of him? Otherwise I can stay," he offered, but he clearly was hoping he didn't have to. He had one foot out the door already.

She smiled. "I'll be fine. Besides, I owe him."

Tripp laughed at that. "Okay, if you need anything, give one of us a call. Got your phone?"

She nodded. "It's in the family room. I'll get it for you."

He typed his number into her cell and left.

Chloe leaned against the door and sighed. She didn't know what kind of night she had ahead of her, if Beck would just sleep it off or wake up in the middle of the night. The one thing she was sure of was he wouldn't make a fool of himself the way she had the night of her non-wedding.

After setting the alarm, she headed back to the bedroom to take care of him.

Chapter Eleven

BECK'S HEAD POUNDED like someone played the drums inside his skull. Groaning, he rolled over, immediately regretting the motion. What the fuck had he done last night?

He blinked and his bedroom came into focus. "Thank God." He wasn't in a stranger's bed. Given how he felt this morning and how little he remembered about the evening before, he counted himself damned lucky.

As he lay there contemplating how he'd manage to get up for Advil and water, the events of yesterday came back to him, and he remembered his father's surgery. He reached for the nightstand, where he always kept his phone, and the pounding in his head stopped him. "Shit."

"You're up?" Chloe's familiar voice asked.

"Barely." He couldn't even open his eyes to face her, the throbbing was so bad.

"Here. I have Advil I found in your bathroom and a glass of orange juice. Think you can sit up and take them?"

"Yeah. I'll manage." He inched his head up and pushed himself up until he was leaning back against the headboard. He peeled his eyes open and met her worried gaze.

"You didn't move once Tripp got you onto the bed," she said, holding out the pills and glass. "Here."

He realized he was still in his clothes from yesterday. A glance told him so was she. Accepting the medication, he swallowed both with the juice, drinking slowly, because his stomach was doing somersaults and he didn't want to throw up.

"Thanks," he said, handing her back the glass. She placed it on a tissue on his nightstand. "How's my father?"

Though he'd needed time alone, getting drunk was fucking stupid because he had no idea how his dad was doing after surgery. Jesus, he was so pissed at himself.

She swallowed hard, obviously worried about his reaction.

"Just tell me," he said, then, catching his angry, misdirected tone, modulated his voice. "Please."

"Well, I'm not sure what you processed yesterday, but despite the change in stages, they're very optimistic. And before you say another word, everyone in your family is on board with the news they heard." She lowered herself onto the bed and sat beside him.

"Everyone hopes you'll come to feel the same way. Your dad needs your support, not worrying about you because you're upset about him."

He nodded. "I know. I was an ass."

She sighed. "No, you were upset and it's understandable. Now you had your night, pull it together and go visit him," she said.

He grinned at her no-nonsense tone.

"What's so funny?"

"Our roles have reversed. You're taking care of me." If only he didn't like it so much.

She looked at him warily. "That's what you do when you love someone, Beck."

He stared at her in shock, waiting for her to take back her words, but she didn't. She stared at him, that damaging phrase dangling between them.

"Chloe, no."

She raised her eyebrows. "Oh? You're going to tell me what I can and can't feel? I have enough of that with my brothers."

He swallowed hard, but his mouth was dry like cotton and his lips almost stuck together. "You don't love me, Chloe." If he said it enough times, maybe he'd convince her. Then this panic running through his veins would disappear and they could go back to the way things had been before.

"You can't tell me what I feel," she repeated, rising

to her feet. Arms wrapped around herself, he saw how much he'd hurt her, but he had to make her understand.

"Chloe, I rescued you after you were rejected by your fiancé. We had fun together. I was there to cheer you on and watch as you started to rebuild your life. But I was just the right guy at the right time to make you feel good. But that's not love. It's rebound."

She stared at him with tears in her eyes. "Good to know how you feel, Beck. You realize that even if you aren't in love with me, if you keep pushing people away, you're facing a pretty lonely life." She turned and walked out, pulling the door shut behind her.

He watched her go, his heart shredded inside his chest. Needing to remind himself why he'd just hurt her so badly, hurting himself as well, he reached over, opened the top drawer in his nightstand, and pulled out the laminated paper with his sister's handwriting.

His sister was gone. Her promised positive outcome had never happened. His dad had stage two cancer, not stage one as they'd thought. Once again, the doctors had been wrong.

He looked down at the list. *Fall in love and get married.* He ran his finger over the words and shook his head. No. He couldn't let Chloe in. Couldn't add her to the small group of people he already had wrapped in cotton in his head and prayed every day he wouldn't lose.

If he could just make her see that he was right, she'd still be his friend. They could still look out for each other but from a distance. And it would be good.

Wouldn't it?

★ ★ ★

CHLOE CLOSED HERSELF in her room and didn't come out until the next morning. She ate a protein bar from her purse for breakfast and used the time to pack everything she'd bought since she moved in. Thank God she'd bought suitcases in preparation for when she left. Her heart was breaking but she had no one to blame except herself. Beck had been one-hundred-percent honest from day one. Falling for him was on her.

Saying *I love you* to him had been a mistake, but she wasn't going to apologize for her feelings or, worse, deny them once they were out there. He was too afraid of losing people to see the truth in front of him. He might not have wanted a relationship but they'd had one. Did he love her? That she didn't know. But he had no right to tell her she didn't love him or make light of her feelings.

"Rebound, my ass," she muttered, zipping up her cosmetics case and finishing up her packing.

The last thing she wanted to do was leave Beck

and the loft that had become her safe haven. She didn't want to move in with Jordan and Linc, but she needed to be in the city, not an hour away at her mother's. So she called Xander, and he'd willingly agreed to let her stay at his apartment uptown. As was typical, Xander was out at the Hamptons house anyway. Still, he promised to meet her at his apartment around ten with a spare key.

She'd called Linc and asked him to do his due diligence on the condo that interested her, but until she had a place of her own, she'd be at Xander's.

She waited until Beck left for work before coming out of her room. His steps had echoed down the hall, and the beep of him unsetting the alarm sounded throughout the apartment.

Once she was alone, she called for an Uber and headed uptown. At least it was just Xander she'd be dealing with and not Linc. She'd just gotten her oldest brother to ease up on Beck, and when he found out about the end of their friendship/relationship/whatever the hell it had been, he'd lose the restraint he'd promised. Chloe wished she didn't have to leave, but she had too much pride to stay.

She'd held herself together all last night and this morning. She was okay while her bags were loaded into the trunk of the car and as she climbed into the back seat. But as soon as she shut the door behind her, the tears began to fall.

★ ★ ★

CHLOE MET XANDER at his apartment. Without asking questions, he told her to make herself comfortable and helped her drag her bags into the spare bedroom. It had closet space, and she didn't want to take over her brother's master bedroom in case he wanted to stay over. He'd left her alone to unpack, and eventually she heard voices in the outer rooms.

She stepped into the hall and headed to the living room, where, sure enough, she found Linc and Jordan with him. "Really?" she asked Xander.

He shrugged. "Linc happened to call while I was on my way to the city."

"So you just had to tell him." She glanced at her oldest sibling. "Did you come to gloat? To say I told you so?"

Linc's compassionate gaze met hers, and she was taken off guard by the kindness in his eyes. "I never wanted you to get hurt."

She blinked back the tears that threatened to fall again. "Well, it's not like Beck didn't warn me, you know? He said he didn't do relationships, had no intention of falling in love, and would never marry. He was pretty specific, so I have only myself to blame for letting myself fall for him."

"I'm not sure you can control who you fall in love with," Jordan said softly, glancing up at Linc.

He nodded, his expression grim.

"But you can go into things with your eyes open and still have the rug ripped out from under you," Xander muttered.

Sasha Keaton, Chloe thought. The famous actress who graced every red carpet, fashion magazine, and social media outlet these days. She and Xander had met before she'd become the It girl, and her brother had fallen hard and fast.

But Sasha had been younger than him and eager for stardom, and though Xander was in love with her, she'd broken his heart. Despite being a former marine with a tough exterior, Xander had a soft inside, and despite the trying to make it work, her ambition and the transient lifestyle had been too much. The breakup had gutted him. Years had passed and he hadn't been serious about any woman since.

Unfortunately her brother's words made a lot of sense. "I know what you mean," Chloe said. "I can't blame Beck just because I fell in love with him." Her eyes filled and she swiped the moisture with the back of her hand.

"Are you sure it was love?" Linc asked. "I mean, you were getting married to someone else a couple of weeks ago. Maybe it's just–"

"Don't you dare say rebound," Chloe said, stepping into her brother's personal space. "I may have had my head in the sand about Owen, I admit that, but I spent time figuring out that I only wanted to marry him because I thought he'd be a safe choice. A man who wouldn't cheat like Dad did." She couldn't contain the snort that escaped. "Clearly I was wrong about that. Just like I was wrong in trying to keep my life choices risk free."

She glanced up at her family, who stared at her and just listened, something she appreciated. "Since Owen dumped me on my wedding day, I've done my best to understand myself and my choices and decide what I want for the future. And Beck was there, helping and encouraging me every step of the way. I know exactly what I feel for him, and I know that it's real. He just doesn't return my feelings."

"He told you that?" Linc asked.

She sniffed and nodded.

"Did he say he didn't love you?" he pushed.

She shook her head. "He said he won't ever fall in love or get married. He's afraid of losing someone the way he lost his sister, and that's not something I can change. Now instead of revisiting my humiliation, I think I'm going to take a walk."

"Want company?" Xander asked.

She glanced at him, surprised. He didn't like the city streets, the noise, or the clusters of people. "Sure. That would be great." With Xander, she could walk in silence and think. Her brother wasn't the type to talk for the sake of filling the silence.

She turned to Linc and Jordan. "Thank you for coming over. Just give me some time, okay?" She needed to lick her wounds in private, and though Linc never meant to push, that was his nature.

"I'm sorry I didn't see you were unhappy with your job and that I didn't give you what you needed creatively." Linc pulled her into a hug. "I owe Beck something for encouraging you. But I'd like to kill him for hurting you."

She laughed. "Let's go back to you two keeping a respectful distance. I think that suits everyone much better than any interaction between you."

"Sure." He stepped back and took Jordan's hand. "Ready?"

She nodded. "Call me if you want to talk," Chloe's soon-to-be sister-in-law said.

"I will."

Chloe spent the day with her brother, but she couldn't get Beck out of her mind.

★ ★ ★

BECK SAT AT his desk, staring at the closed door he

knew wouldn't be opening so Chloe could pop her head in. He'd left her at the apartment this morning, walking out early so they could avoid an awkward morning. He wasn't sure why he thought going home tonight would be any easier, but oh, well. He'd just have to face her then.

They'd go back to being roommates and friends, if they could get past the uncomfortable fact that they'd slept together and she'd admitted to having feelings for him he just could not handle.

He groaned and buried himself in work, calls, meetings, anything he could do not to think. By three p.m., he headed over to the hospital to see his father in person. He'd already checked in this morning and midday. Despite normal post-operative pain and issues, his dad seemed to be in an upbeat mood and was trying to recuperate fast by doing everything the doctors instructed. He wanted out of the hospital ASAP. Not that Beck blamed him.

Not wanting to tire his father out, Beck didn't stay long, but the doctors said he was supposed to go home Monday if he had a restful weekend with no issues. And they should have biopsy results by the end of next week. He pushed that thought away and headed home.

Braced for a discussion of some kind, he entered the loft, which seemed strangely quiet. The lights inside were off, which was unusual considering Chloe tended to sit in the big family room with the lamps on so she could read.

Hoping like hell she hadn't retreated to her room, he put his phone on the credenza and walked down the hall. Her door was open but her lights were also off.

His gut churning, he looked inside. The room was empty. Devoid of the perfume she kept on the dresser, the bottle of water on the nightstand, and other odds and ends he'd gotten used to seeing there. He stepped into what he'd come to think of as Chloe's room and opened each dresser drawer, finding one after the other empty. And though he knew what he'd find, he checked the closet anyway. Everything that belonged to her was gone.

"Fuck." He lowered himself onto the bed and ran a hand through his hair. Had he really expected her to stick around after his rejection? He'd been deluding himself all day because he hadn't wanted to consider the possibility that she'd move out without a word.

The hell of it was, he couldn't blame her.

His cell rang, and he walked out of the empty bedroom and headed to the entryway, where he'd left the phone. A number he didn't recognize flashed on the screen, and though he'd normally ignore it, something told him to answer.

"Hello?"

"Hey, asshole. Meet me at the club in thirty minutes. We need to talk."

Beck closed his eyes and groaned. "Linc, do we really need to do this tonight?"

"I can't think of a better time. See you then."

Knowing he was going to get his ass handed to him, he debated not showing up but then decided enough time had passed. The least he could do was hear Linc out.

No matter what the other man had to say.

★ ★ ★

BECK WALKED INTO the club he'd last been at with Chloe, deliberately late. If Linc was going to rip him a new one, at least he'd know he couldn't order him around and expect immediate compliance. Sometimes it was the little things that helped a man maintain power.

He arrived to find the other man sitting at a private table in the corner with a bottle of Macallan and two lowball glasses.

Beck lowered himself into the empty seat across from him. In silence, he poured himself a drink, glanced at Linc, who merely nodded. He tipped the bottle and watched the liquid rise, finished, and slid the glass across the table.

They each picked up a glass and took a long sip.

Linc studied him, rolling the glass between his palms. "I was drunk but it was no excuse. You were my closest friend and I betrayed you."

Beck blinked. He'd expected to be slammed about how he'd treated Chloe, not receive what was as close to an apology as he was likely to get.

"I'm not saying this to excuse my behavior, but I have a rough memory of a woman crawling into bed with me saying, 'I'm back.' I thought it was Lacey, too drunk to process that it wasn't." Linc dipped his head, his regret more than clear.

"Shit." Beck didn't know what to say. He'd had no idea Jenna had pretended to be Linc's girlfriend. His stomach churned at what Linc must have been feeling. If things had been the other way around, Linc would be in jail. There were words for women like Jenna. He shook his head.

After all these years, Beck wouldn't just take the apology, he'd give Linc a little more than his understanding. "Jenna was a bitch. I watched her make her way up the food chain at school. You were a means to an end. She wanted more of my time and used you to try and get it. When I didn't quit my job, she moved on." Beck shrugged. "It wasn't easy to get past back then. Later on, it always seemed too late. The anger and hatred between us festered over time and land deals."

"Agreed. Now answer a question for me. Did you use my sister to get back at me?" Linc took another big gulp.

"Fuck no." Beck raised his glass and paused. "Although that first morning, I can't say I didn't enjoy watching you lose your shit."

Linc rolled his eyes and Beck couldn't withhold a grin.

But his smirk disappeared when he thought of Chloe. Sliding his hand off the glass, he curled his hands into fists. "Nothing I did for your sister had anything to do with you."

It had everything to do with the sad female in the wedding dress trying to pretend alcohol made everything okay. Then he'd seen the real woman who'd fallen apart upstairs in the hotel suite, and something about her called to him.

He often thought she reminded him of who his sister might have been. A strong woman surrounded by brothers, struggling to make her own way. But Whitney never had that chance. And he wasn't going to open himself up to anyone, not even the beautiful, gutsy Chloe Kingston.

"Yeah, I know you didn't use her," Linc said.

That shocked him. But before he could speak, Linc continued.

"What I'm trying to say is, I came to understand you weren't using her. At lunch, Chloe told me how much you supported her, encouraged her, and were there for her in a way I couldn't be…" Linc ran his hand over his eyes, his frustration with himself showing. "I didn't know what my sister needed. She kept her unhappiness hidden. I had no clue she found her job unfulfilling. And no matter how many people told her she was making a mistake with Owen, she wouldn't admit she chose him for the wrong reasons."

Dammit. Beck actually felt sorry for his old friend. He'd feel the same way if it were his sister and he'd missed all the signs of her distress. "It's easier for an outsider to see things," he said, actually attempting to make Linc feel better.

"Well, regardless, you got her to open up and made sure she followed her dreams. I'm grateful and it's not easy to admit that to you." Linc leaned forward in his chair. "But what I'm not happy with is the fact that she moved out of your apartment because you were a fucking asshole to her."

"And there's the jerk I know. Welcome back," Beck muttered. But he couldn't help but ask, "How is she?" He'd been thinking about her nonstop, hating himself for hurting her and frozen inside, unable to thaw and reach for what he really wanted.

"How do you think she is? But she's tough. She'll

get over you," Linc said oh so easily.

Ouch. The thought of Chloe moving on made him want to puke, but he forced himself to remember his reasons. "Look. You want what's best for Chloe and so do I. The one thing we can agree on is that's not me." It couldn't be him.

"As much as it galls me to admit this, you're wrong," Linc said. "She loves you and thinks you can make her happy. From what I've seen, she's right."

That Linc, of all people, was pushing him toward Chloe was a shock. Still, Beck shook his head, not wanting to delve into his past and his pain with anyone. But he owed it to Chloe to explain it to someone who could help her get through this.

He finished his drink for fortification and put the glass down on the table. "You know about my sister."

Linc nodded. "And I know that's why you've shut Chloe out. I just think you need to reconsider. You're denying yourself happiness out of fear. I can tell you from experience, love is worth the risk."

"Loss isn't and that's not something you've experienced yet. And I don't wish that on anyone. Including you." He refilled his glass.

"Well, at least I can say I tried." Linc leaned back in his chair, a disgusted look on his face. "But you're the same stubborn asshole you've always been," Linc said but his smirk meant he wasn't serious. He clearly didn't like Beck's choices but knew they were his to make.

Beck lifted his glass and treated Linc to the same grin. "Back at you, buddy," he said and took another drink before sliding his chair back and heading home.

★ ★ ★

CHLOE MADE IT through the long weekend, in part because Xander stayed in the city instead of heading back to his beach house. He didn't want to leave her alone, and she was grateful for the company. They hung out, binge watched television, ordered in pizza and ice cream, and just had a chill couple of days.

She missed seeing her brother, and spending time alone together was special. She heard all about his upcoming movie. Of course, she'd already read the book, but she enjoyed hearing about the script alterations that were made and the reasons for changing it compared to the novel. But no matter how much Xander tried to distract her, she couldn't forget Beck.

After talking and seeing him daily, she hadn't heard a word since she'd moved out. She had no idea how he'd felt about coming home to find her gone, whether he'd been relieved he hadn't had to ask her to leave or sad to lose what they'd shared.

It was crazy how they'd bonded so fast, during such unusual circumstances, and she wished things could be different. But not having him in her life didn't mean she wasn't concerned about his family, especially his father. She had Tripp's phone number saved and, earlier this morning, called him to get his mom's cell. She checked in without discussing anything about Beck. His mom didn't ask, and she didn't offer information about why she wasn't getting her follow-ups from Beck himself.

Despite being miserable and missing Beck, Chloe refused to give in to the same melancholy that had pulled her down after Owen left her at the altar. She had goals to focus on and a future to prepare for.

She already knew she'd survived being publicly humiliated and dumped on her wedding day, so she'd somehow get through losing Beck.

★ ★ ★

BECK SPENT THE weekend at the hospital and the office, avoiding his empty apartment, where every room reminded him of Chloe.

Linc's voice echoed in his ear. The unexpected apology. The admission that he felt Beck was good for Chloe. And the disgust on Linc's face when Beck refused to give in and see things the same way.

Monday evening, Beck left work and headed to his parents' house. His dad had been released that morning and spent the day in bed resting. Beck wouldn't stay long, but he needed to see his father for himself and know that he was okay.

He let himself in and found his mom in the kitchen, making chicken soup. After walking over, he gave her a kiss. "Hey."

"Hi, Beck. Perfect timing. Your brothers staggered their visits today, and you're the last one for the night. He's completely up for seeing you." She smiled. "Want some soup?"

"No, thanks. I picked up something and ate in the car on the way here. I didn't want you to have another mouth to feed. You have enough to worry about."

She waved the ladle at him. Soup dripped on the floor and his mom just laughed. "It's my job to feed you. I don't care how old you are."

Beck grabbed a paper towel and wiped up the spill.

"Now where's that beautiful girl of yours?" she asked. "I can't believe how sweet she is. She really took care of us all at the hospital."

He cringed. He hadn't thought his mom would ask about Chloe because she'd be too consumed with worry over his dad. Though he considered fudging the truth, he couldn't lie to his mother. "She moved out and I haven't spoken to her since then."

His mom stopped stirring and grew still. Then she placed the large spoon on the counter, shut the knob on the stove top, and walked over to the kitchen table.

Gesturing to the chairs, she said, "Sit." It sounded like an order and Beck took it as one.

He sat across from his mother and waited for whatever it was she had to say.

"Why?" she asked.

"Why what?" He was playing dumb, but it bought him time to gather his thoughts.

She rolled her eyes. "Don't play games with me, Beckett. Why did Chloe move out?"

Dammit, she'd pulled out the big guns, his full name.

He studied the woman who, in his opinion, was one of the strongest he'd ever met. She'd survived losing a child and managed to hold her family together afterwards.

"Because she told me she loved me and I … I can't say it back." He clasped his hands together in front of him.

His mom narrowed her gaze. "Because you don't? Or because you're afraid?"

When he remained silent, she spoke again. "I saw how you two acted together. The sweet touches, the whispers, the reading each other's mind." She shrugged. "Did I judge you two wrong?"

He swallowed hard and forced himself to face his mother and the truth. "No. You didn't."

Beck had been trying not to replay his talk with

Linc, but one thing kept running through his mind. *You're denying yourself happiness out of fear.*

He absolutely was. And he was pissed at himself for it.

"Okay, honey, listen to me." She leaned forward and put her hand on his. "We all lost your sister." Her voice was shaky but she went on. "We all grieved. And we all moved on because we had no choice. But you … you're stuck in that place where you think the doctors lied and anyone with cancer is going to die. Neither of those things is true."

He dipped his head, unable to speak because she was right.

"They say your father will beat this, and I choose to believe them. Otherwise I'll live in fear and I refuse to do that."

Beck jerked his head up and met her gaze. "How do you do it? Remain so optimistic? Move on?"

She squeezed his hand tighter. "Because the years I had with your sister mean everything to me. Do you think I would give those up even if I knew the ultimate outcome?" She shook her head in reply. "We both know I wouldn't. I had her for sixteen beautiful, wonderful years." Tears fell from her eyes, and she wiped at them with her free hand. "Losing her destroyed me for a while, but I had so much to live for. You, your brothers, your father."

Beck listened to his mother. Really listened. Because he suddenly realized if he didn't, he stood to lose the most precious thing in his life *now*.

Hell, maybe he already had.

"So let me ask you something," his mom said.

He looked at his mother. "How have you been feeling since Chloe left you?" she asked.

"Empty. In pain. I've been doing everything I can not to think about it because I have only myself to blame. But Whitney's always there, stopping me from letting myself feel more," he admitted.

His mother pursed her lips. "Okay, let me ask you a different question. If Chloe died today, would you be relieved you let her go so you didn't feel pain? Or would you feel angry and regret the four days you could have had with her?"

He jerked in his chair, those words finally penetrating the frozen barrier he'd kept around himself. The one he'd tried to use to keep Chloe out. But it hadn't worked. She'd reached inside him anyway and captured the one thing he'd sworn never to give away.

His heart.

He rose to his feet.

"Where are you going?" his mother asked, a knowing smile on her face.

He grinned. "To see Dad. Then I have a couple of things to do tomorrow morning."

"And then?" She stood up, joining him.

"I'm going to get my girl … if she hasn't given up on me."

His mom smiled. "Good. Because the other thing I know is that Whitney would never have wanted you to live your life alone. And by the way," she called out to him.

He turned back toward her.

"I think Chloe will cut you some slack for being stuck in the past."

He hoped like hell his mother was right. Because even if he deserved to have Chloe turn her back on him, he couldn't handle losing her forever.

Chapter Twelve

BECK WALKED TO his sister's grave and sat down beside the gray stone. The sun shone overhead, the day fitting his positive mood. He no longer had a weight sitting on his chest, and he had his mother and her opening up about love and life to thank for the profound shift. He'd let her talk about his sister, and he'd listened instead of tuning her out or storming off because he didn't want to face the pain.

Beck held the laminated paper and a spoon in his hand. He wasn't one for talking to someone who was no longer alive, but he believed his sister was aware of his feelings and the changes inside him thanks to their wise mother.

She had made him see some truths he never would have realized on his own. Losing Chloe already hurt. Coming home to an empty apartment and discovering he'd driven her off had felt like he'd taken a sledgehammer to his heart, and he damned sure regretted every second since he'd rejected her. If something happened to her, he'd be just as devastated whether they were in a relationship or not. He was wasting precious time being alone and hurting the woman he loved in the process.

As much as it sucked to admit, Linc had also made a valid point. Beck had been denying himself happiness out of fear. It had taken Chloe coming into his life and making herself at home in his heart for him to be willing to listen to his mother for the first time and be able to put the past where it belonged.

Taking the spoon, he dug up a small layer of grass large enough to hold his sister's bucket list, and he placed it in the ground. Then he covered it up again, patting down the earth.

"I know I was putting off completing the end of the list. I didn't want to finish it because it felt like a final goodbye," he said. "But I'm ready now because I did it. I fell in love just like you wanted me to."

He drew a deep breath and went on. "As for getting married, well, we just have to hope I didn't screw things up with Chloe too badly. And if I can make *that* happen, we'll both go see the last item on your list."

Smiling, he placed a hand on the cool stone. "I know you'd love Chloe, too. Just like I know this isn't goodbye because you're always with me." He waited a few seconds longer, heard the chirp of a bird, nodded, and walked off, his head and his heart lighter than they had ever been.

From the cemetery not far from his parents' house,

Beck drove back into the city, to the address Linc had given him. Surprisingly, his old friend hadn't given Beck a hard time when he'd called to ask where Chloe was staying. Linc had, however, warned Beck that this was the only chance he'd get to make things right. If Beck hurt her again, they'd be back to hostile enemies. Beck got it.

He found a parking spot around the corner, not an easy feat in Manhattan in general, and walked to the building. He knew Linc had called Xander ahead of time, and the doorman let Beck head up to his floor, and he knocked on the door.

While waiting for someone to answer, he shifted on his feet, knowing if it was Chloe, he'd be groveling immediately. Anything to undo the pain and damage he'd done.

The door opened and Xander Kingston stood in front of him. He was buffer than Linc and had a full beard covering his face. Even his stance said ex-marine. Apparently being a thriller writer hadn't softened him one bit.

"Beck," the man said, stepping aside so he could enter.

He walked inside, turned, and shook the other man's hand. "Good to meet you. I've heard a lot about you."

"From Chloe." Xander dropped his sister's name

between them, the glare in his eyes matching his expression.

Another Kingston brother ready to kill him, and Beck couldn't even blame him. "Is she here?"

Xander cocked an eyebrow. "I heard the shower go on a few minutes ago. I'm sure she'll be out soon."

"You didn't give her a heads-up that I was coming?" Beck asked.

Xander shrugged. "I figured it would give you and me time to talk. This way." He tipped his head, gesturing for Beck to follow.

He ended up in a nice-size kitchen, seated at a round table, Chloe's brother staring at him. Unsure what to say, Beck remained silent.

"Well?" Xander finally asked.

"Well, what?"

"Why are you here? Unless it's to apologize and grovel, I suggest you leave before Chloe comes in." Xander leaned back in his chair, looking comfortable and relaxed.

But his tone was anything but and extremely familiar. "You sound a lot like Linc. And for what it's worth, I plan on doing whatever I need to in order to get her back."

Beck ground his teeth, wishing he didn't have to go through Chloe's brothers to get to her. But having just left his sister's grave, he respected these men and their loyalty to their siblings.

"You'd better hope Chloe's more forgiving than I was."

Beck's stomach twisted at the thought of Chloe not giving him a second chance. Instead of focusing on the negative, he latched on to something Xander had said. "More forgiving than you were. Sounds like you have an ex out there who screwed you over."

He didn't expect Xander to elaborate, but the other man leaned forward in his seat, elbows on the table. "When I got my first movie deal, I was out in LA, and I got involved with someone just starting out, too. An actress."

"Anyone I'd know?"

Xander met his gaze, paused, then said, "Sasha Keaton."

"Holy shit," Beck muttered. She was a hot commodity in show business.

"Right. Except she wasn't a name then. Just a girl I fell for, but she wasn't the person I thought she was." He shrugged as if it meant nothing, but a muscle ticked in his jaw, and Beck knew whoever this woman was, she meant something to Xander Kingston.

"I won't hurt Chloe again," Beck said.

"You'd better not. I may sound like Linc but I have a much better right hook." He didn't look like he was joking, either.

"Understood."

"Beck?" Chloe's voice had him standing and turning to face her.

She stood in the entry to the kitchen, her eyes wide as she stared at him, blinking as if she couldn't believe he was here and not some figment of her imagination. She wore a pair of leggings and an oversized tee shirt that fell just above her knee. *His* shirt. And since he couldn't read her expression, he chose to take hope from her choice of clothing.

"And that's my cue to leave." Xander rose from his chair and glanced at Beck. "I meant what I said."

"Never thought you didn't," Beck muttered, done with the Kingston brothers' posturing. Although given Xander had opened up to him, he understood where the man was coming from.

"What's going on?" Chloe asked.

"You have a visitor." Xander kissed her cheek. "I have a feeling you won't be needing me anymore, so I'm going to get some things together and head back to the Hamptons. You can stay here as long as you want, but if you go, keep the key." He glanced at Beck. "Just in case."

He walked out, leaving them alone with Beck feeling as if the life he wanted was on the line.

★ ★ ★

CHLOE LET HER brother leave, using the time to gather herself before turning back and meeting Beck's gaze. She'd woken up this morning to the sun streaming through the window, but her mood hadn't matched the beauty of the day. She'd wondered if subconsciously she'd been holding out hope she'd hear from Beck by now, because no matter how hard she tried, each day away from him had been more and more difficult. She'd told herself to give up.

Now he was here, looking handsome in his jeans and a black tee shirt, tempting her with what she couldn't have. And it hurt.

"Can we talk?" he asked, breaking the silence.

"Sure." She took a step into the kitchen, planning to sit at the table.

"Somewhere more comfortable?" he asked.

Chloe nodded, leading him to the family room with a U-shaped sofa and two large club chairs with ottomans. The emotional distance between Chloe and Beck was tangible, and she was tempted to sit in one of the chairs and keep herself safe. In case he just wanted to talk and end things on a friendly note. Nausea filled her at the thought.

No sooner had she taken a step than Beck grabbed her hand and pulled her toward the sofa, bracing his hands on her shoulders.

"I need you close." He swallowed hard. "To say

what I have to say, I need you here."

At his admission, she dropped to the couch and took a seat.

He blew out a relieved breath, settling in beside her. "I fucked up. When you told me how you felt, when you said that you loved me, it scared me, so I played dirty. I threw your life back in your face and dismissed your feelings like they were nothing more than a stupid mistake." Reaching out, he grabbed her hand and pulled it onto his thigh. "I'm sorry."

His touch felt too good and his words were just that. "Is that why you're here? To apologize? Fine. I accept your apology but I wish you'd sent a text or an email." Anything that wouldn't have gotten her hopes up, and she attempted to yank her hand away, but he held on tight.

"Can I finish before you rip into me?" he asked.

She forced herself to relax, listen, and not jump to conclusions. "Go on."

"I love you, Chloe."

She stilled, certain she'd heard him wrong. "You love me. As in…"

"Cross-it-off-the-bucket-list love you. Yes." He rubbed his thumb over the back of her hand. "But I couldn't handle it. I was afraid to admit it and petrified about possibly losing you, too, one day."

At the mention of his sister, she lifted her head and

met his gorgeous green gaze. "What changed?" She wanted to understand and needed proof he wouldn't panic later on and push her away again.

"I went to see my parents last night. Dad got out of the hospital yesterday," he said.

She nodded. "I know. I spoke to your mom around lunchtime."

"You did?" he asked, obviously surprised.

She couldn't believe he'd think she could walk away like he had. "Just because we aren't together anymore doesn't mean I don't care about them. I wanted to know how your dad was doing."

"Thank you," Beck said, his expression soft and filled with gratitude.

This Beck was so easy to love, and her heart pounded in her chest, suddenly filled with hope.

He stared into her eyes. "Mom had a lot of wise words. Things I should have listened to years ago but I…" He shook his head. "I wasn't ready to hear."

"And you are now?"

"I am," he said with certainty in his tone.

Certainty that had her believing.

"Your brother and I met up… We made some sort of peace. And he also helped me see I was pushing you away out of fear."

Chloe's eyes watered. Nothing made her happier than her brother and Beck calling a truce.

"Then Mom asked if I was hurting without you." He now held both her hands in his. "And she wanted to know if something happened to you, if I'd be in any less pain because we weren't together, and in that moment, everything crystallized. I can't be without you. I need you in my life because I love you."

Everything he said made such perfect sense, and tears filled Chloe's eyes, blurring her vision. She knew how much pain his sister's death had caused him, and the fact that he was able to come to her this way meant the world to her.

"I love you, too, Beck. So much." She threw herself into his arms and pressed her mouth to his.

He wrapped his arms around her, hauling her against him, and she shifted until she was settled in his lap, her knees on either side of his strong thighs, her sex grinding against his hard erection. His tongue slid past her lips, and she finally felt like she was home.

"Hey, kids. Give me a chance to get out of here first, will you?"

Chloe pulled back and glanced at her brother. He passed through, a duffel bag over one shoulder as he headed out.

She grinned. "Bye, Xander. Thanks for everything."

"You're welcome, sis. Any time." He paused and looked past her to Beck. "Take care. I'm assuming I'll be seeing you around."

"Count on it," Beck said and laughed.

Xander walked out, the door shutting behind him.

"Know what I really want to do?" Beck kissed her neck.

"What?" she asked, knowing she'd do anything he wanted.

"Pack you up and take you back home where you belong."

She leaned into him, breathing in his familiar and arousing scent. "I want that, too. But I know what I'd rather do first." With that, she maneuvered off his lap and tugged him to his feet.

Once back in her room, she began to undress, Beck doing the same, when she caught sight of her cell with a voicemail alert on the screen. Something made her pick up the phone, open the voicemail app, hit play, and put the phone to her ear to listen.

Shirt already off, Beck paused, watching her and waiting.

A female voice spoke, and Chloe's hands began to shake as the words sunk in. "Oh my God. I won! I won the Elevate contest! I'll be overseeing the opening of their New York office." She tossed the phone onto the bed.

Before she could blink, Beck was beside her, picking her up and spinning her around. "I am so damned proud of you." He kissed her hard and fast. "Do you see how far you've come?"

"You were there for me, understanding what I needed before I did. Supporting me when I needed it. And believing in me."

He grasped her hands. "Right back at you, Chloe. We make a perfect team." He scooped her into his arms and placed her down on the bed.

Clothes flew and then they were naked, Beck on his back, Chloe's knees on either side of him as she grasped on to his erection. Thick and smooth in her hand, she settled him at her entrance and slid down, taking him deep inside her.

His gaze hot on hers, he gripped her hips with his hands and held her tight as she lifted herself up and down, riding him, keeping them joined tight. And it wasn't long before Chloe felt that familiar stirring inside her.

"God, Beck, I'm so close." She slammed down, rocking her hips forward before rising and repeating the motion.

"Then come, princess. Come for me. I'll be right there with you."

His desire-filled command worked, and her climax erupted, everything inside her soaring. And just as he promised, he thrust up and stiffened, his orgasm hitting at the same time as hers. Together in a way she knew would last forever.

A little while later, she lay in his arms, his fingers trailing over her skin. "I know you were looking at apartments. Do you like the loft?" he asked.

"I love it. Is it too soon to say it feels like home?"

"Once you're moved into my room and make it *ours*, then it's home."

She rolled over and pressed her lips to his chest. "I don't think I could be happier," she murmured. "We have to tell our families the news."

He laughed. "Something tells me Xander already knows and is spreading the news as we speak."

"True."

"We can tell my parents when we visit my dad later if you want to come with me."

"Of course I will," she said.

"Good." His fingers grazed over her arm. Goose bumps formed and arousal peaked once more, but then she realized something important. "Beck, we didn't use protection … but I'm safe and on the pill."

"I'm safe, too, and I'd never put you at risk." He paused. "Do you want kids?"

"I do. Very much. Just not right now. After I've had some time with my career, I'd love to have children." She froze, realizing that maybe after losing his sister, children weren't something he wanted in his future. "Do you?"

He flipped them over until he was on top of her. "I want to make you happy, Chloe. As many kids as you want, I'm in."

She smiled, wondering how life suddenly got so good. And she was very grateful Beck had rescued her when she was at her lowest. Because together they were at their very best.

Epilogue

Two Months Later – Summer

CHLOE WATCHED DASH and the Original Kings play a song he'd written just for Linc and Jordan on their wedding day. Her famous brother, always the fun player, flirted with the single women when he wasn't on stage.

"I know they wanted a small, intimate wedding but this is actually nice," Chloe said to Beck, who stood with one arm wrapped around her waist.

"It is. Your mother can be persuasive when she wants to be."

Chloe laughed because her mom had been the reason for the change in wedding plans from a small family gathering to a last-minute bigger event. After all, she hadn't gotten to celebrate her daughter's wedding the first go-round.

The band announced a break. The guys dispersed to get drinks to cool them off, and Dash headed straight for a woman he'd been obviously eyeing all night.

"He's going to get himself in trouble one day,"

Chloe said, her gaze on her brother.

Beck nodded. "I hope he doesn't have to learn the hard way that variety is not the spice of life."

"It's a good thing you realize that," she said, playfully poking him in the ribs and looking into his eyes.

"I only need you, princess." He dipped his head and kissed her on the lips. "Are you sure you aren't upset about that Page Six article online?"

She shook her head. "The main focus was on Linc and Jordan's wedding. But I admit them writing about a potential merger between two Manhattan real estate dynasties if we got married was funny. It's like reading about strangers. They don't know us at all."

They weren't even engaged, and with everything happening in their lives, Chloe was okay with that. They were taking their time, enjoying being together without fear hovering between them. Even Beck and Linc were taking steps toward reconciliation, and Chloe was grateful.

"Good. Because the only thing I care about is if they're hurting you," Beck said, a sexy, protective glint in his eyes.

"I'm fine. I promise."

He grinned. "Then let's dance." Beck led her out to the dance floor and pulled her tight against his tuxedo-clad body.

"Did I mention how hot you look?" She stared up

at him, lost in those emerald-green eyes.

"Can't say I mind hearing it. But you look exquisite, and I look forward to peeling that dress off you later."

Her heart skipped a beat and arousal settled low in her belly. "Can we leave soon?" she asked, eager to be alone with him.

He shook his head. "Not until the bride and groom take off. Wouldn't want to give Linc a reason to be pissed at me."

She treated him to a pout. "Like he'll notice who's there to wave them off." But she pressed deeper into Beck's embrace and enjoyed the rest of the day.

She hadn't been lying when she told him she was good. Beck's dad was doing well—the surgery had gotten all the cells, no spread into lymph nodes, and in the end, he hadn't needed chemotherapy after all.

Chloe had started working for Elevate and had been given all the freedom she needed in hiring designers, choosing clients, and setting up their new office downtown. Keeping busy during the day, going home to Beck at night, she was in a better place than she'd been in a very long time.

★ ★ ★

BECK THOUGHT THE newly married couple would never leave the reception. Knowing Linc, he was stalling on purpose to torture Beck one last time. But finally, Jordan changed from a beautiful bride to a woman ready to head to her honeymoon. They were headed to the Greek islands while a pregnant Jordan could still travel.

Linc and Jordan stopped by Chloe and gave her a hug.

"I'm so happy for you two. Go have fun and we'll see you when you get home," she said.

"Maybe the four of us can get dinner," Jordan said, and she and Chloe laughed.

Beck broke the ice first. "I'd like that." He hoped he and Linc could get back to what they once had. With the past rehashed and hopefully left there and Linc's blessing for what Beck planned to do next, it remained a possibility.

Linc grunted and Beck laughed. "I'm taking that as a yes. Have fun," he said.

The couple said their goodbyes and took off in a white 1930s Touring Rolls Royce rented convertible, and the wedding guests made their way back inside.

The band took the stage. Meeting Beck's gaze, he tipped his head.

Beck turned to Chloe. "I'll be back in a second. Stay put, okay?" He didn't want her disappearing into the ladies' room and being missing when he needed her.

She nodded and sat down in a chair.

Beck made his way to behind the stage, meeting up with Dash and Xander. Aurora and Melly, Chloe's mother, had been alerted and were sitting at their seats near the stage.

To Linc's credit, upon hearing Beck's plan, he'd suggested Beck arrange for his parents and brothers to come after he and Jordan left. If they'd been invited to the actual ceremony, Chloe would know something was up, and Beck wanted this moment to be a complete surprise. Damn Page Six for alluding to the moment, but he still didn't think Chloe had a clue.

Dash pulled out the box he'd stashed somewhere safe and handed it to Beck. "Good luck," he said, slapping him on the back. "And take care of my sister."

Beside him, Xander's expression said all Beck needed to know. It was going to take some time to warm up to the more solitary of the brothers.

He glanced out into the audience and saw his family standing in the back, which meant this was his cue. He didn't want Chloe to catch sight of them first.

"Ready," he said to Dash.

The lead singer headed up on stage and took the mike. "Thank you all for coming tonight. Before we get to the last set before the festivities end, we have something special for you first." He gestured toward the side of the stage, and Beck squashed his nerves and walked out to join him.

Taking the mike from Dash, he turned toward the guests, focusing on a wide-eyed Chloe, who obviously had no idea what was about to happen.

"Since today was Linc and Jordan's wedding, I didn't want to do anything to take away from their moment, but as the oldest Kingston brother, I did need his blessing, which he gave me."

"It's contingent," a familiar voice said from the back of the room. "Treat her right and we'll be fine."

Beck narrowed his gaze. He hadn't expected Linc to come back.

"Do you really think we'd miss this? We circled back around and snuck in. And no, you're not taking anything from our day. Now get on with it."

Chloe rose to her feet. "What's going on?" she asked, her cheeks flushed.

Beck handed Dash the microphone and took the few steps from the stage to the dance floor. "Chloe, I could think of only one way to prove to you that you're it for me forever. Both of our families are here to see this."

She gasped and looked around, her eyes wide when she turned back to him.

He strode up to her and dropped to one knee. He'd already waited long enough and cut to the chase without flowery words that weren't him. "Chloe Kingston, I love you and always will." He opened the velvet box. "Will you marry me?"

She didn't even look at the ring he'd had made special for her, merely throwing herself into his arms and saying yes, over and over as he held on to her tight.

Finally he couldn't wait another moment and whispered in her ear. "Don't you want to see the ring?"

She pulled back, tears falling from her eyes. "I already have what I want." She looked into his eyes, her happiness something he shared. "But of course I do."

She looked inside the box and squealed with utter glee. "It's a princess cut!"

He grinned. "You're damned right it is. Because you're my princess." Taking out the ring, he slipped it onto her finger. "They say it's the most brilliant cut of all diamonds and you deserve it. And every time you look at it, you'll know you're mine."

A round of applause followed and he rose to his feet. Then they were surrounded by family and friends wishing them well.

Beck's brothers pushed their way through to welcome their new *sister* to the family.

"Just what I needed. More brothers!" Chloe exclaimed, then hugged each of them, who she'd already formed tight bonds with.

His parents came next, then Chloe's mom and sister, with her baby in her arms. Once they'd been duly congratulated and Beck had been warned again not to hurt the woman he loved, everyone finally dispersed, leaving Beck alone with his fiancée.

He loved the sound of that word.

Pulling her into his arms, he said, "I can't wait to make you Chloe Daniels."

She grinned. "Maybe we can get away with the smaller, intimate wedding."

They glanced at their mothers, who had their heads together, no doubt planning already. "Or maybe not," he muttered but his smile remained.

The only person standing alone was Xander, making Beck wonder if the other man would ever put his hurt behind him and move on. The way Beck had.

"Let's go home and have our own private celebration," Chloe said.

He picked her up and carried her out of the room. Just the way a princess deserved.

Xander Kingston's latest novel is being made into a movie, and when the female lead is cast, how will the former Marine turned thriller writer handle having the woman who betrayed him back in his life?

Order JUST ONE CHANCE!

He thought she was the one . . . until she walked away. Now she's back and he wants her more than ever.

As a former Marine, Xander Kingston's writing keeps him sane. Bonus? His thrillers made him one of Hollywood's most desired screenwriters – and also introduced him to a fledgling starlet who broke his heart. With his close-knit family in New York, Xander returned home and found peace. Until Sasha Keaton shows up at his Hamptons retreat. Now an A-Lister, she's as beautiful as he remembers. And just as dangerous to his heart.

Sasha learned from watching her mother to never sacrifice her dreams for anyone—only to discover how empty life could be without the man she loved. Now cast in Xander's latest movie, she needs his insight to play the part, but secretly hopes for a second chance.

Xander has built emotional walls to keep Sasha at a distance, but their physical attraction can't be denied. When a stalker's threats intensify, Xander moves Sasha into his house to keep her safe. Before long she's back in his bed and making inroads in his life.

But when the danger passes and the movie wraps, Sasha and Xander face a familiar choice—put career first or give love a fighting chance.

★ ★ ★

About the Author

NY Times, Wall Street Journal, and USA Today Bestseller, Carly Phillips gives her readers Alphalicious heroes to swoon for and romance to set your heart on fire. She married her college sweetheart and lives in Purchase, NY along with her three crazy dogs: two wheaten terriers and a mutant Havanese, who are featured on her Facebook and Instagram. The author of 50 romance novels, she has raised two incredible daughters who put up with having a mom as a full time writer. Carly's book, The Bachelor, was chosen by Kelly Ripa as a romance club pick and was the first romance on a nationally televised bookclub. Carly loves social media and interacting with her readers. Want to keep up with Carly? Sign up for her newsletter and receive TWO FREE books at www.carlyphillips.com.

Made in the USA
Coppell, TX
03 July 2021

58552626R00148